Prizm Books

Aisling: Book I Guardian by Carole Cummings
Aisling: Book II Dream by Carole Cummings
Aisling: Book III Beloved Son by Carole Cummings
Changing Jamie by Dakota Chase
City/Country by Nicky Gray
Comfort Me by Louis Flint Ceci
Desmond and Garrick Book I by Hayden Thorne
Desmond and Garrick Book II by Hayden Thorne
Devilwood Lane by Lucia Moreno Velo
Don't Ask by Laura Hughes
The End by Nora Olsen
A Field Guide to Assassins of Muromachi Street
by Tamara Sheehan
Foxhart by A.R. Jarvis
Heart Sense by KL Richardsson
Heart Song by KL Richardsson
I Kiss Girls by Gina Harris
Ink ~ Blood ~ Fire by K. Baldwin & Lyra Ricci
Josef Jaeger by Jere' M. Fishback
Just for Kicks by Racheal Renwick
The Mediocre Assassin's Handbook by Tamara Sheehan
The Next Competitor by K. P. Kincaid
Repeating History: The Eye of Ra by Dakota Chase
The Strings of the Violin by Alisse Lee Goldenberg
The Suicide Year by Lena Prodan
Tartaros by Voss Foster
The Tenth Man by Tamara Sheehan
Tyler Buckspan by Jere' M. Fishback
Under the Willow by Kari Jo Spear
Vampirism and You! by Missouri Dalton
The Water Seekers by Michelle Rode
The World's a Stage by Gail Sterling

Tyler Buckspan

Jere' M. Fishback

Tyler Buckspan

This is a work of fiction. Names, characters, places, and incidents either are the product of the author's imagination or are used fictitiously. While this novel is inspired by historical events, it is a fictionalized portrayal, and the author created all characters, events and storylines in the pursuit of literary fiction, not historical accuracy.

Tyler Buckspan
PRIZM
An imprint of Torquere Press, Inc.
PO Box 2545
Round Rock, TX 78680
Copyright 2013 © by Jere' M. Fishback
Cover illustration by Fiona Jayde
Published with permission
ISBN: 978-1-61040-518-8
www.prizmbooks.com
www.torquerepress.com

First Prizm Printing: August 2013
Printed in the USA

there's room under the rainbow

www.prizmbooks.com

Tyler Buckspan

Jere' M. Fishback

Tyler Buckspan

CHAPTER ONE

On a summer afternoon in 1963, a pickup with missing hubcaps and a cracked windshield left my half brother Devin at the curb in front of Grandma's house. Heat radiated from the asphalt road when Devin leapt from the truck's bed. He waved thanks to three men wearing straw hats who occupied the truck's cab. A pair of boxer shorts peeked from a grocery sack Devin carried in the crook of his arm. While the truck rattled off, he stood on the sidewalk, gazing at the house and using his hand as a visor. He worked the concrete with a sneaker toe.

Lanky and dark-haired, Devin was nineteen years old. His blue jeans sagged. His underwear showed, and his tight-fitting T-shirt was dark in the armpits. In one rolled-up sleeve, he stored a pack of cigarettes.

I sat on a glider sofa in the shade of our front porch, staring at Devin. A *Green Lantern* comic book rested in my lap, and I clutched a glass of iced tea.

"Who are you?" he asked.

"Who are you?" I answered, even though I knew.

I'd never met Devin, but Mom had told me all about him. A product of her first marriage, Devin was a high school dropout. He'd spent a year in a Georgia state prison, following an arson conviction. Just before his release, Mom had paid Devin a visit, up in Georgia, the first time they'd spoken in many years.

Now Devin would live with us.

"I don't know for how long," Mom had told Grandma over supper the previous evening. "The boy needs *someplace* to stay until he's situated."

My grandmother blinked behind her bifocal lenses. "I don't see why he can't live with Gordon, like before."

Gordon was Mom's *first* husband. My dad was number two.

Mom set her fork on her plate. Placing her elbows on the table, she glared at Grandma.

"I told you: Gordon and his folks have washed their hands of Devin."

"With good reason: he's a criminal and a mischief-maker. Do you think for one minute you'll change that?"

"I can try," Mom said.

Grandma shook a finger.

"The first sign of trouble, he's out the door. Understood?"

Now, Devin climbed the steps and approached me. Extending his hand, he told me his name. His long eyelashes and turned-up nose gave his face a girlish look, but his grip was firm, his voice deep for a guy his age. Like me, he spoke with a North Georgia accent.

I didn't rise when we shook. I only told him I was Tyler.

He asked, "How old are you?"

"Fifteen. I start high school—ninth grade—next week."

He narrowed his emerald eyes.

"You look younger, like you're fourteen."

Great. Why did people always say that? I wasn't as tall as some guys my age, and I was skinny, but I grew hair in all the right places. During summer break, I'd performed push-ups each morning, before breakfast. I started with two sets of twelve. Now, I was up to three sets of twenty-five, and it showed in my chest and shoulders.

Well, *I* thought so anyway.

Devin stared through the screen door, into the house. The bag in his arm crackled.

"Is my mom home?"

"She's on the job; so's Grandma."

My mother worked in Daytona Beach, as a stylist in a beauty parlor; she trimmed hair, did perms, color jobs, and manicures.

"I hate it," she'd told me countless times. "I'd do anything to escape that place."

Mom was petite, a slender woman with dark hair and eyes, copious makeup, and a nasal voice that quickly sharpened when something displeased her. She subscribed to a half dozen movie magazines. Often, she'd daydream out loud after reading an article about Ava Gardner or Elizabeth Taylor.

"Imagine being a film star," she'd once told me. "I'd spend my days sunning myself beside a swimming pool in Beverly Hills, or I'd live in Malibu, overlooking the Pacific. I'd do all my shopping at Neiman-Marcus and never *touch* a hair curler again."

My grandmother was a self-employed medium in Cassadaga, our tiny community in northeast Florida. In a cramped storefront, she read tarot cards. She conducted séances where she spoke with the dead. She also read palms and offered advice. A dozen other Cassadaga women did so as well. Believers came to our town from all over the southeastern United States, seeking spiritual guidance from the "gifted ladies."

"Don't tell your grandmother this," Mom had once told me, "but I think spirituality's bunk, a complete fraud."

Now, on the front porch, I set down my tea glass and comic book. Then I led Devin inside.

Built before the First World War, my grandma's house was wood-framed and two-storied, with a tin roof, heart of pine floors, two wood-burning fireplaces, and dormer windows extending from each of five, second-floor bedrooms. A man six feet tall could stand up straight in the attic. Grandma favored walnut furniture, damask drapes, and Oriental carpets. Sloping roof eaves kept every room dark, even at that hour, despite a plethora of double-hung windows. Aromas of mildew and mothballs permeated the place.

I slapped our lion's head newel post before leading Devin up the stairs. The treads creaked while we rose. Devin's tobacco-scented breath swept my neck. His body odor smelled like spoiled milk, and I crinkled my nose.

Don't they have toothpaste and soap in prison?

"This'll be yours," I said, leading him into the smallest of our bedrooms. An iron framed, three-quarter bed, painted in black enamel and draped with a chenille spread, hugged one wall. A bureau with a hazy mirror occupied a corner. Cobwebs swayed in several places where the water-stained ceiling met the walls. A dead cockroach lay upon its back, on a braided area rug.

After opening the closet door, Devin sniffed and shook his head. He opened the dormer window, sat on the bed. The springs beneath him wheezed. Setting down his grocery sack, he produced a lighter with a hinged lid. Then he reached for his cigarettes.

"You shouldn't smoke in the house," I said. "Grandma won't like it."

Shrugging, he lit up and inhaled. Then he blew a stream of smoke. It burned my lungs and made me want to cough, but I didn't let myself. The bluish haze rose to the ceiling, where the smoke hovered among the cobwebs.

I pointed to Devin's left hand.

"What are those marks?"

After he raised his arm, I stepped forward for a closer look. His first name, written in squiggly blue font, appeared on his thumb and fingers, one letter per digit.

"It's a prison tattoo; I did it myself."

I nodded and moistened my lips. "What's it like when they lock you up?"

He shrugged. "You wouldn't care for it: all these smelly, stupid guys. The food's lousy and the screws bully you; they—"

"Screws?"

"It's what we call the guards. Some are okay, but most are cruel bastards, and they're all on the take. For a price, you can get anything you want in prison: booze, drugs, even sex."

I arched my eyebrows.

"They bring women inside?"

Devin looked at me and grimaced.

"Not *that* kind of sex. Use your imagination."

I blushed. Lowering my gaze, I shifted my weight from one leg to the other.

Devin cleared his throat.

"Like I said, you probably wouldn't like prison."

He drew on his cigarette. Then he made an "O" with his lips and blew smoke rings. The rings floated over my head while I cracked my knuckles, trying to think of something to say. Several seconds passed. Then Devin broke the silence.

"So, what's a guy do for fun in Cassadaga?"

I chuckled and shook my head. "There's a fresh water spring, half a mile from here; it's nice for swimming. Otherwise, you take a bus to Daytona; you watch a movie, go bowling, and stuff like that."

He rose and took a last drag off his cigarette, before

flicking the butt out the window. Exhaling smoke, he turned to me and pointed toward Grandma's free-standing garage. Above its opening hung a plywood backboard with a basketball goal, a Christmas gift from my mom I had rarely used.

"Got a basketball?" Devin asked.

My grandma kept a quart-sized water jug in her Frigidaire. Now Devin and I passed it back and forth, seated on the rear steps of Grandma's house. We had both removed our shirts; we used them to mop sweat from our faces. I studied Devin's physique while he raised the jug to his lips, and his Adam's apple bobbed. His chest and shoulder muscles were defined, his biceps too. His belly was flat and striated, his nipples dime-sized and chocolate-colored. The hair under his arms was dark, like that on his head.

We had played four rounds of "Twenty-One," and Devin smoked me every game. His movements on the driveway were quick and precise; his jump shots were works of art. He dribbled behind himself, between his legs, running circles around me. He almost never missed a lay-up.

Now, on the steps, he told me, "Ball handling's the key to winning; keep your opponent guessing. Move fast and mix things up."

There were no boys my age in Cassadaga; the town was an old folks' community, I explained to Devin. My experience with competitive basketball was limited to pickup games at school. My skills, I told him, were dismal.

"We'll work on that," Devin said. Then he poked my shoulder with a finger.

"What?" I said.

He sniffed his armpit. "I'm hot and smelly. Why don't we visit that spring you told me about?"

My pulse quickened, and a smile crept onto my lips.

Tyler, you have a brother now.

Life had grown more interesting.

CHAPTER TWO

In 1948, when my mother divorced Devin's father, Devin was four years old. Mom declined custody of Devin, leaving him in the care of his dad and paternal grandparents. They lived in the north Georgia town of Dahlonega.

"I know it seems strange," Mom had once told me, "a mother leaving her son like that. But my nerves were shot at the time; I couldn't handle the responsibility."

I said, "How come you never visited him? Why didn't he ever visit us?"

"I *did* visit once, up in Dahlonega, just before Devin started kindergarten, but it didn't go well. You see, Gordon's parents, Dee and Herbert, never liked me. They poisoned Devin's mind, told him all sorts of lies about me."

"Like what?"

Mom raised a shoulder. "It doesn't matter. But when I visited up there, I tried to hug Devin. He cursed a blue streak and kicked my shins so hard they bled. After that, I kept my distance from him."

Back then, her divorce may have jangled her nerves, but despite this, Mom found herself another husband within a year: Roger Buckspan of Decatur, Georgia, the man who later sired me. My dad managed a legion of Amway salesmen, and we never lacked for skin care products or household cleaning solutions. His income, combined with Mom's beauty shop earnings, kept us comfortable in our rented bungalow.

Dad even owned a financed car, a used 1952 Oldsmobile Super 88 with a Rocket Power V8 engine, a convertible roof, turquoise paint job, and white sidewall tires. I loved riding about the streets of Decatur on summer evenings, with the top down. Wind blew through my hair, and glow from streetlights reflected in the Super 88's shiny hood.

While watching Dad Simonize the Oldsmobile in our carport one Saturday, Mom stood at a window and crossed her arms beneath her breasts. Then she shook her head. "I often wonder," she said, "if he loves that car more than you or me."

The Super 88 had problems. Its carburetor was finicky, and the engine had a tendency to stall out at inconvenient times. The engine also suffered from vapor locks, so if Dad turned off the ignition on a warm day, sometimes we'd wait forty-five minutes for the Rocket Power V8 to cool, before Dad could restart it. When this happened, my dad would curse General Motors, Georgia summers, and the Lord himself. He'd pound on the steering wheel while the Super 88 stubbornly refused to turn over. The car wouldn't make a sound when he turned the key, and we'd all sit there, sweating on the vinyl upholstery.

The Super 88's maladies were, in fact, the cause of my dad's untimely death.

On a July afternoon, when I was eight and the sun broiled Decatur's thoroughfares, the Super 88 stalled out while Dad crossed railroad tracks near the intersection of North McDonough Street and East Howard Avenue. According to eyewitness statements, Dad repeatedly tried starting the car, without success. A Seaboard Air Line passenger train approached while onlookers hollered at

Dad to exit the Super 88.

"It seemed like the driver was glued to his seat," one woman told a stringer for the *Atlanta Journal Constitution*. "He kept turning the key over and over, but the engine seemed dead as a doornail."

Another witness said, "The conductor blasted his horn, more than once. Still, that crazy fellow wouldn't budge."

Dad's funeral was, of course, closed casket. A spray of roses and carnations, paid for by Amway, draped the coffin. The company's emblem appeared among the blossoms. Five dozen Amway salesmen attended the service—stoop-shouldered fellows in alpaca business suits, wearing skinny neckties and scuffed brogues.

Unable to make ends meet on her beautician's income, Mom brought us to Cassadaga, where we had lived ever since, in Grandma's house. Mom hated the place; she called it "the sticks." She told me, "I'd give anything to live elsewhere, but right now it's not possible."

As I'd explained to Devin, Cassadaga was an old folks' community, so I attended elementary and junior high schools in nearby Orange City. Now though, I would attend high school in the town of Deland, seat of government for Volusia County.

I'd grown up without playmates, spending most of my free time reading books. Hardy Boys detective novels and Civil War history volumes were among my favorites. I'd solve crossword puzzles or play solitaire. Sometimes, I wandered through citrus groves, listening to the buzz of honeybees and inhaling the sickly sweet smells of orange blossoms while searching for arrowheads and shards of Indian pottery. On warm days, I often visited the spring I had told Devin about. I also kept a diary, at Grandma's suggestion; I made entries before bed each evening.

"I've done it since I was a girl," Grandma had once

told me, shortly after we moved in with her. "Reflecting on events of your day makes life more meaningful. And it's fun—every so often—to pick up an old volume, to see what you were up to, many years before."

I had recorded my own impressions and activities in spiral notebooks for three years now. Already I'd filled a half dozen notebooks; I kept them hidden beneath a stack of sweaters in my bedroom closet.

In the fall of my sixth grade year, three years after we'd moved to Cassadaga, I contracted encephalitis, presumably from a mosquito bite. I was hospitalized with a high fever. They pumped me full of antibiotics. Then I was quarantined at home for weeks. I had no appetite and lost fifteen pounds; I looked like a scarecrow. I became so weak I barely made it to the bathroom to pee. I spent my days reading *World Book Encyclopedia*, making it all the way through the "R" volume within six weeks.

By the time I recovered, I was so far behind in school my principal decided to hold me back a year; he placed me with the fifth graders. I didn't mind, really. Thereafter, I was the oldest kid in my classes. I'd always been small for my age, and for the first time in my life, I wasn't the classroom shrimp.

My grandma didn't own a television set. ("There's nothing but trash on TV.") Her console RCA radio, with its glowing tubes and bulky white knobs, picked up Orlando and Jacksonville stations playing *Grand Ole Opry* or Lawrence Welk, and I rarely listened to it.

When Devin arrived in Cassadaga, my life there had been lonely and dull.

But now, as I prepared to visit the spring with Devin, I asked myself: *Are things about to change?*

CHAPTER THREE

After slipping between two courses of barbed wire, Devin and I trudged down a path bisecting a forest of slash pines. Above us, squirrels barked and hopped about branches. Both of us were shirtless; we carried bath towels draped over our shoulders. Dappled sunlight reflected in Devin's hair. Our sneakers crushed pine needles, and a sharp odor of tree sap scented the air.

"This is private property, owned by a lumber company," I told Devin. "I've been here dozens of times, but I've never seen another person."

The spring was pod shaped, maybe the size of two tennis courts. Its sandy bottom was white as table sugar, the water clear. Sunlight reflected in the spring's placid surface. Devin sat on the trunk of a fallen pine tree, next to his towel. He removed his shoes and socks while I stood motionless, watching him. After standing, he reached for the button at his waist, popped it open, and ran down his zipper.

Already, my pulse raced.

Devin shucked his jeans to his ankles, kicked them off, and placed them next to his towel on the tree trunk. Then he looked at me and crinkled his forehead.

"Aren't you going to swim?"

I nodded. Leaning against the pine trunk, I unlaced

a sneaker, my hands shaking. I glanced up, just in time to see Devin lower his briefs, and what I saw made my mouth turn pasty.

Holy crap...

I returned my gaze to my shoe, afraid I'd pop a boner if I didn't.

Minutes later, we stood waist deep in the cool spring water, both of us naked. Sunlight glanced off our shoulders. Devin did the talking; he spoke of north Georgia, about prison and so forth.

I listened, fascinated.

Devin's physical presence and the sound of his voice had my heart racing. I'd never been alone and naked with another guy before. To me, the situation seemed reckless and intimate. I studied Devin's chest and arm muscles, his collarbone and the curve of his neck, where it met his shoulder.

I raised my chin, squinted at the sun.

He's beautiful, was all I could think.

So beautiful.

"I don't cotton to cigarettes," my grandma told Devin, while she passed me a bowl of turnip greens that night at dinner, "especially not in the house. If you must smoke, keep a coffee can on the back steps. Do your puffing there."

We sat at the dining room table: Grandma, my mom, Devin, and I. Early evening sunlight entered through the western windows, reflecting off a monogrammed silver water pitcher; the pitcher rested on a cork coaster. A platter of baked ham and a bowl of mashed sweet potatoes steamed on the table, alongside a silver breadbasket and a butter dish. Odors of reduction and oxidation chemicals wafted from my mom's beauty shop uniform.

My grandma presided over dinner in her usual attire: silk blouse, strand of cultured pearls, wool skirt, stockings, and shoes with heels the size of a toddler's building blocks. Her ample breasts jutted like a ship's prow. Each week, Mom would style Grandma's nickel-colored tresses, using plenty of hair spray. You'd have needed a chisel to budge a ringlet on Grandma's head.

Devin didn't smell anymore. He'd styled his hair with Amway hair tonic, borrowed from me; the tonic reflected the glow from my grandma's chandelier. He wore a collared Banlon shirt—a welcoming gift from Mom—and his chest muscles showed beneath the slinky garment.

I wore my usual attire: T-shirt with horizontal stripes, blue jeans with the cuffs rolled, and high-top canvas sneakers. I had styled my hair with tonic as well.

Mom said to Devin, "A customer of mine, Sarah Parnell, says her husband's hiring laborers at his brickyard. It's tough work and pays only minimum wage, but it's a start. She'll put in a word if you'd like."

Devin nodded.

Grandma added her two cents.

"The county offers adult education classes, evenings at the high school in Deland. You can earn your GED there."

Devin studied his plate while a crease appeared between his eyebrows.

"Something wrong?" my grandma asked.

Devin looked at me, my mom, and then Grandma.

"I never cared for books," he said.

My grandma snorted; her pearls rattled when she rearranged herself in her chair.

"Education's essential to a young man's career. You don't like money? Don't you want to own a car and buy a home?"

Devin lowered his gaze, said nothing.

Grandma continued. "How will you support a wife and children? Toting bricks?"

Devin twirled his fork in his fingers. He raised his chin and looked at Grandma.

"Maybe," he said, "I'll earn a living like you do."

My grandma's eyebrows rose. She opened her mouth, but before she could say something, Devin spoke.

"That woman you saw today—the one from Ormond Beach? I could've talked to her dead boy just as well as you, maybe even better. And now you have twenty-five dollars in your purse, for just an hour's work. It sure beats brickyard labor."

Grandma's eyes bugged while her jaw sagged. She sat motionless, staring into Devin's face.

"I don't like this," Grandma told my mother. "Something's fishy."

I stood outside my grandma's bedroom door, eavesdropping.

"He clearly has a gift," Mom said of Devin, "probably passed down from you."

In the hallway I puckered one side of my face. *A gift?* Hadn't Mom once called Grandma's spirituality "bunk" and "a fraud"?

An hour before, Devin had communicated with Grandma's late husband, Elmer, dead twenty years. We sat in Grandma's parlor—Mom, I, and Grandma—while Devin stood before the fireplace, head bowed.

Devin said to Grandma, "Elmer wants you to know he forgives you for selling his horse—the black mare named Penny—when he lay in the hospital."

Grandma grew ashen-faced. Looking at Mom, she

said, "Your father wasn't working, and we needed money. I didn't have a choice."

"And speaking of money," Devin said, "Elmer says there's a Prince Albert tobacco tin buried east of your gardenia bush, about a foot deep, near the corner of the house. Money's stored there for a rainy day."

Devin shared lots of information Elmer had provided him: the date Elmer had proposed marriage to Grandma *and* the location (an ice cream parlor in New Smyrna Beach), the name of a hotel where Elmer and Grandma had honeymooned in Savannah, and the name of another boy who'd competed with Elmer for Grandma's affections. All the while, Grandma sat in silence on her horsehair sofa, hands in her lap, her eyebrows knitted.

Afterward, I held a flashlight while Devin shoveled dirt. My grandma and Mom stood beside us in the dark, arms crossed at their bosoms, while fireflies darted here and there. The Prince Albert tin was rusted, but still watertight. When Devin pried the lid open, the flashlight's beam fell upon a wad of ten dollar bills.

Now, in Grandma's bedroom, Mom said, "You're not happy about the money?"

"Well, of *course* I am, but... let me ask you something."

"What?"

"Before this evening, how much had you told Devin about me and your father?"

A bedspring creaked.

"Nothing, really," Mom said. "When I spoke with him at the prison, I mentioned your work. I told you were widowed, that's about it."

No one said anything for several seconds.

I shifted my weight from one leg to the other, chewing a hangnail. Then I heard a pair of knees crackle.

Grandma said, "I don't trust that boy."

CHAPTER FOUR

I'm not sure when I first suspected I was gay; probably when I had to shower with other guys in my junior high school's locker room. Every time I gazed at a cute guy in his birthday suit, my mouth grew sticky. I tried ignoring my feelings—I pretended they did not exist—but lying in bed at night, I'd stare at the ceiling while visions of naked boys crowded my thoughts.

When Devin came to Cassadaga, I still hadn't confronted my homosexuality; I wouldn't allow myself to think of myself as queer. But now, a month after Devin's arrival, I couldn't deny my urges any longer.

I'd fallen hopelessly in love with my half brother.

I found his green eyes enchanting, his voice hypnotic, and his muscles arousing. One afternoon, when I came home from school to an empty house, I crept into Devin's room. After rummaging through his clothes hamper, I found a filthy pair of briefs he'd worn to his job at the brickyard. I took the reeking, skid-marked garment to my room. Then I sat on my bed and brought the shorts to my face. I inhaled Devin's myriad of scents, while my heart thumped and I touched myself until I reached orgasm. I nearly passed out during the process—no joke—and afterward I stowed Devin's briefs under my mattress, already looking forward to future sniff sessions.

How wicked, I thought while I cleaned myself up. *What kind of a pervert am I?*

At dinner that evening, my cheeks burned when I looked across the table at Devin. I recalled his stinks and the way they had excited me. Now, I felt a stiffening between my legs. Devin looked up from his plate, his gaze met mine, and then he crinkled the corners of his eyes, as if he knew my deepest secrets.

I couldn't look him in the eye. I lowered my gaze and swallowed.

Had Devin just read my thoughts? Did he know I'd romanced his underwear?

If so, how?

On a Monday evening in early November, the Cassadaga Council of Mediums gathered in Colby Memorial Temple, for public discussion of my half brother and his purported powers. The main question: should the council permit Devin to offer his services as a medium to the public, under the council's auspices?

Without the council's blessing, no one in Cassadaga would rent business space to Devin. My grandma had already declared Devin couldn't work out of her home, no way. So Devin was at the council's mercy.

A dozen women, all ordained by the Spiritualist Church, sat on folding metal chairs in a circle, some my grandma's age, some younger. Devin sat among them, wearing dress slacks, a Banlon shirt, and leather slip-ons. His hair reflected light from an overhead fixture. His hands rested in his lap, and he spoke softly when answering the council's questions.

When had he first realized he had a gift? What technique did he use to make contact with beings in the "spirit world"? Had he seen visions? Had he ever predicted future events with accuracy?

Mom and I watched from a bench at the rear of the room. The room wasn't air-conditioned; the place felt stuffy, and my armpits dampened. Mom dabbed her upper lip with a hanky.

"As a young teenager," Devin said, "I had visions. I heard voices speak to me but was too immature to understand. I sensed I was different, but I didn't know exactly why or how."

Rev. Gloria Hagermann, the council's chairwoman, leaned forward in her chair. Squinting her eyes, she spoke in staccato. "You understand, our members won't tolerate chicanery. We won't allow exploitation of folks who come to us for guidance, not in Cassadaga. If you want to be a fortune teller with a neon sign and a crystal ball, open shop in Jacksonville."

Devin lowered his gaze and kept quiet.

Rev. Hagermann addressed my grandmother. "Louise, the boy's been under your roof a while now. Tell us, is he genuine? Has he a true gift? Or is he looking for easy money?"

While Grandma rearranged herself, her pearls rattled. "I want everyone to know I'm personally opposed to Devin's request. He's young and inexperienced. I fear trouble will come if he serves as a medium."

"Do you doubt his ability to contact the spirit world?"

Grandma spoke of Devin's communications with my grandfather. She talked about the Prince Albert tin, explaining the situation in detail. "I'm still not sure what to think of it all."

Rev. Hagermann turned her gaze back to Devin. "I understand you recently spent time in prison."

Devin's cheeks colored, but he kept his chin high. "That's right," he said.

"For what reason?"

"I set fire to my father's house."

The room fell silent. I looked at my mother, but she wouldn't look at me.

No wonder he couldn't go back to Dahlonega.

Rev. Hagermann tugged at the hem of her skirt. "Would you care to explain *why* you committed such a crime?"

Devin lowered his gaze and worked his jaw from side to side. Then he looked at Rev. Hagermann.

"My father molested me sexually, as a child."

Rev. Hagermann's hands flew to her face, while several women gasped.

I squirmed in my seat. For the first time, I realized Devin might carry any number of secrets from his past. What kind, I didn't know, of course. But I really didn't know Devin well, did I?

"I set the fire for revenge," Devin said, glancing about the room, "and I don't regret it. I'd do it again if I had the chance."

Rev. Hagermann squared her shoulders. "Have you committed other crimes?"

"No, ma'am, I have not."

"Has your grandmother acquainted you with the council's Code of Ethics?"

Devin nodded.

"And?" the reverend asked.

Devin said, "They seem sensible and fair."

"You understand, don't you, that you must apprentice with a council member for three months? You'll have to earn her blessing, before you can work alone."

Devin said he knew that.

Rev. Hagermann's gaze traveled about the circle. "Do I hear a motion on this matter?"

Rev. Grace Patterson—a petite woman in a sleeveless

blouse, culottes, and sandals—raised her hand. I looked at her painted fingernails and her heavy mascara, and then I thought of something my grandma had once told my mother about Rev. Patterson, at our dinner table.

"I've known Grace Patterson all her life. She and Helen Hagermann, Gloria's daughter, were best friends as children. Both turned boy-crazy when they came of age; you never saw such goings on. Helen took up with a hoodlum from Orlando, a boy who rode a motorcycle. One night he raped Helen, and then he stabbed her to death in an orange grove. She was only fifteen."

My grandma had clucked her tongue. "Grace Patterson may be ordained, but she's a nymphomaniac. I've heard stories about her affairs: the postman, the mechanic at the Sinclair station. Why, even her idiot gardener's a victim. She only gets away with these things because she's the richest woman in Cassadaga."

Now, Rev. Patterson told the council, "I move we permit Devin to serve an apprenticeship." She swung her gaze to my grandma. "What harm can it do?"

"Who will Devin train under?" Grandma asked.

Rev. Patterson beamed at Devin. "I'm *happy* to work with him."

My grandma grunted and shook her head.

"Do I hear a second?" Rev. Hagermann asked.

"Second," another woman said.

"All in favor?"

Eleven hands rose, including Rev. Hagermann's.

But Grandma's hands remained in her lap.

CHAPTER FIVE

On a Saturday afternoon in November, I worked a crossword puzzle, seated on Grandma's sofa, when a knock sounded at the front door. An auburn-haired guy Devin's age stood on the porch. He held a rolled-up blanket under his arm; a six-pack of beer dangled from his fingertips. His cheekbones were prominent, his deep-set eyes cobalt blue, his skin was light as ivory.

"Devin home?" he asked in a scratchy baritone.

After I let him in, I pointed to the staircase.

"Second room on the left."

Minutes later, the two descended, Devin clutching bath towels and his cigarettes.

"Tyler," he said, pointing his thumb at the other guy, "this is Jesse. He works with me at the brickyard."

Jesse raised a palm.

Jesse was slim like Devin, about the same height, also dressed in jeans, sneakers, and a T-shirt.

"We're going for a swim," Devin said. "I'll see you later."

Through a window, I watched them walk down the sidewalk, conversing and laughing, both smoking cigarettes. Right away, I felt jealous. After all, *I* was the one who'd shown Devin the spring. He should only bathe there with me, not this Jesse guy, right? I moistened my lips, watching Devin's behind twitch in the seat of his jeans. My hands hung at my hips and my fingers flexed. Would the two of them get naked? If so, what would Jesse's body look like?

Go ahead, chickenshit. Why not find out?

I snagged my jeans on the lumber company's barbed wire fence, wincing when I heard the denim rip. The jeans were new—intended only for school—and I'd surely receive a tongue-lashing from Mom when she saw the damage.

Damn.

For mid-November, the weather was steamy. My armpits moistened as I crept along the path leading to the spring. Sunlight filtered through trees; it warmed my shoulders. The only sound I heard was the crunching of pine needles beneath my sneakers. Rain had fallen the night before, and now the forest smelled of wet bark and damp earth.

I hadn't visited the spring since I'd taken Devin there, and the memory caused a tingle in my briefs. I'd only seen him naked that one time.

I came to a tree felled and blackened by a lightning bolt. The trunk was as big around as an oil barrel. This meant the spring was only twenty or thirty yards ahead. After leaving the trail, I took care when parting undergrowth, trying to be quiet. I made my way toward the spring, bending forward at the waist and keeping my head low. Already, my pulse quickened. I'd never spied on someone before, and the thought of peeping at Devin and Jesse seemed deliciously wicked.

I expected to hear their voices when I drew close to the spring, but I didn't, and then I crinkled my forehead in puzzlement.

Why weren't they talking? What were they up to?

I passed through a bank of saw palmettos. Sunlight glittered on the spring's surface. Above me, a squirrel barked on a limb; its bushy tail twitched. I straightened my spine, pulled aside a palmetto frond, and....

Jee-zus.

Devin and Jesse were naked, about thirty feet from me. Droplets of spring water glistened on their skins. Their hair was damp, but they were not bathing, not now. They lay upon Jesse's blanket. Their heads bobbed, and their lips smacked. A handful of Jesse's auburn hair fell across his face, waving like a flag when his head moved.

My knees weakened while my breathing accelerated and sweat trickled down my ribs; I had never seen such a thing. I watched in fascination for several minutes, licking my lips and flexing my fingers. What must their bodies feel like? What thoughts dwelled in their heads? And weren't they ashamed? Wasn't their brand of sex an abomination?

I unbuttoned my jeans and lowered the zipper, taking care not to make any noise. Then I spit in my hand and touched myself, my gaze fixed upon Devin and Jesse. I felt more sexually excited than I'd ever been. Both guys were handsome, their bodies lean and muscled. I especially liked Devin's buttocks; they were round as melons, porcelain white, and I longed to touch them.

Devin brought his face to Jesse's, and their mouths met. For the first time in my life, I saw two males kiss. The vision made me shudder, and I longed to trade places with Jesse.

What does it feel like, having sex with another guy? Especially when you're in love with him?

When I reached orgasm, I felt as if someone had nudged me with a cattle prod. Purple spots appeared before my eyes; I gasped for air and my scalp prickled. I had never, *ever* experienced such excitement.

I stood there, catching my breath and shaking my head in wonderment. *I've just witnessed a secret ceremony of sorts: the kind most people wouldn't even try to understand.*

I closed my eyes and swallowed.

One day I'll taste another guy's skin and lips, I know I will.

Okay, all right...

At the spring that November afternoon, Devin had given himself to Jesse. But while my breathing slowed and my body relaxed, I knew Devin had shared something special with me as well.

He had given me—the queerest of boys—a glimpse of what I needed to be happy.

The next day, my mom drove Grandma to visit a relative in St. Augustine; they left at sunrise. After breakfasting alone, I lay on my bed in my underwear with my back propped against the headboard. I was reading a *Time* magazine when Devin entered, yawning, his dark hair in tangles. Like me, he wore nothing but a pair of jockey shorts. The bulge of his genitals made my heart gallop. I swallowed and tried not to stare. Inside my underwear, I stiffened.

Devin sat on the edge of the bed, near my knee. I smelled his skin and morning breath, while the bedsprings creaked. He took the magazine from my hands. After glancing at the article I read, he closed the *Time* and placed it on my mattress.

"You know," he said, "if you're going spy on folks, you should be more careful."

Oh, shit.

I opened my mouth, planning to deny everything, but Devin raised a palm.

"If Jesse had known, he'd have kicked your ass into next week."

I nodded, thinking, *No doubt.*

"Did you enjoy watching us?"

I nodded again. My mouth tasted like it was full of pennies.

"Ever had sex?"

I shook my head while my heart thumped.

Devin's gaze met mine. "You're a good-looking boy, Ty. I'm sure it'll happen soon enough."

I found my voice, though it cracked when I spoke. "How about now? We're alone and—"

Devin shook his head. "You're underage. I don't feel like going back to prison."

"I won't tell anyone; I can keep a secret."

"No, Ty. I mean it."

A lump formed in my throat. My eyes watered and my chin quivered.

"What's wrong?" Devin asked.

"You think I'm just a kid."

Devin placed a hand on my thigh. "You're not a child, I know. But wait awhile longer, before you have sex."

"Why?"

"I started too young; people hurt me. Don't make the same mistake."

I sniffled and didn't say anything. I wanted Devin. Why didn't he want me?

He patted my knee.

"Is there anything you want to ask?"

Go on.

"Is Jesse your boyfriend?"

"I guess."

"Do you like him?"

Devin bobbed his chin. "He's nice-looking, don't you think?"

Nodding, I shifted my buttocks on the mattress. "How did you know I was there yesterday?"

He brought an index finger to his temple. "I have extrasensory perception—ESP. Heard of it?"

I shook my head.

"I'm aware of *all* that happens around me. When you snagged your jeans on the barbed wire fence yesterday, I knew it."

Shit.

I said, "What else do you know about me?"

Devin flickered his eyebrows.

"I know you like the smell of my dirty underwear."

I looked away, cheeks flaming, eyes watering anew. I'd never felt more embarrassed in my life.

"Ty, it's nothing to be ashamed of. Boys do that sort of thing."

A tear slid from a corner of my eye, then another. Sniffling, I crossed my arms at my chest and gazed at the ceiling.

"Look at me," Devin said.

I did, blinking more tears.

"Anytime you have a question—or whenever you have a secret to share—you can always come to me. I spent time in prison; nothing will shock me. Understand?"

I nodded, rubbing my eyes with the heels of my hands.

"Was it true what you told Reverend Hagermann?"

"What's that?"

"Did your father... mistreat you?"

He nodded.

"How old were you?"

"He started when I was ten. It wasn't fun."

I shuddered.

Devin drew a breath, and then let it out.

"Any other questions?" he asked. "I mean it, you can ask anything."

I shook my head.

CHAPTER SIX

Florida's warm weather continued into the third week of November. Most days, I wore T-shirts or Banlon pullovers to school, and my PE classes were sweaty affairs. The air in our locker room was so humid my clothes stuck to me like a second skin, after my shower.

Friday, November 22, I stood at the pencil sharpener in my afternoon Geometry class, just after lunch. The room was not air-conditioned, and sweat beaded on my upper lip when the room's intercom speaker crackled. I crinkled my forehead. Normally, the intercom system was used for morning announcements or fire drills, nothing else. What was going on?

Our principal was always a vibrant man—a guy ready with a wisecrack—but now he cleared his throat a time or two before speaking in a husky voice.

"Students, faculty, and staff, I regret to inform you that our President, Jack Kennedy, has been killed by a gunshot wound in Dallas, Texas. The party responsible has not been identified. Vice-President Lyndon Johnson has already been sworn into office as our new president.

"President Kennedy's body will be flown to Washington, where his funeral will be held next week. I would ask that each of you offer a prayer for President

Kennedy's family, and for our nation.

"God bless America."

I felt like someone had slapped the back of my head with a two-by-four. My mind went blank, and my lunch roiled in my stomach. My knees quivered like a guy dancing the Jitterbug. A vision of Kennedy came to me: his handsome face, his shock of brown hair, and his dazzling smile. I recalled how his broad shoulders filled out his tailored suits, and how gracefully he moved through a crowd. I remembered the speech he'd given, announcing commencement of the "Space Race" between our country and the Soviet Union, which had transformed nearby Brevard County from a sleepy coastal community into a beehive of aerospace activity. I recalled Kennedy's Boston accent and his wry sense of humor when he answered questions during press conferences. And, of course, I thought of his steadfastness during the 1962 Cuban Missile Crisis, when we all held our breaths until Russian ships, bearing ICBMs as cargo, turned around in the face of America's naval blockade.

Kennedy had always struck me as an invincible guy, a man above the fray, an insider with all the answers, but now he was dead, just like that.

My vision fogged while I stumbled back to my seat. My mouth tasted like I'd swallowed something nasty, and my stomach kept doing flip-flops. How could Kennedy disappear from our lives so suddenly? The whole thing seemed ludicrous. If the President wasn't safe from danger, who was?

The rest of the day went by in a blur. Girls wept in the hallways, and teachers spoke to one another in hushed tones. All sorts of crazy speculations bubbled up. Some said Castro had hired the assassin, to avenge the Bay of Pigs invasion Kennedy had supported. Others said Nikita Khrushchev had instructed the KGB to kill the president.

Some believed Lyndon Johnson had hired the assassin so he could succeed Kennedy in office. And others thought the killing was the work of white supremacists who hated Kennedy for his support of the Negroes' civil rights movement.

Although I'd never paid much attention to politics, I tended to suspect the latter theory. Kennedy had never been popular in northeast Florida. Nixon had carried Volusia County handily, and he won Florida's ten electoral votes as well, albeit by a narrow margin. Even after the election, I'd seen crude signs nailed to roadside tree trunks: "Impeach Kennedy", "JFK Loves Niggers", and "The Pope has JFK on a rope."

Some kids left school early that day. Others, like me, eschewed their afternoon classes, instead gathering in the cafeteria, where Walter Cronkite's steady basso offered the latest news on a portable, black-and-white television. Even before I boarded my school bus home, a suspect had been arrested; a ferret-faced guy named Lee Harvey Oswald with a five o'clock shadow, a bruise on his cheek, and a cut over one eyebrow. Cronkite said Oswald had sustained his injuries during a scuffle with police, inside a Dallas movie theater. A rifle was recovered from a school book depository, and a Dallas police officer had been murdered, allegedly by Oswald.

Dinner that night was particularly solemn. My grandmother dabbed at her red-rimmed eyes with her napkin. Mom was tight-lipped, and Devin had little to say as well.

"I didn't vote for him," Mom told us. "I never agreed with much of what he said or did, but still, it's a horrible thing."

I kept my gaze on my plate, pondering the day's events in silence. The whole thing seemed chaotic and nutty, more like a *Twilight Zone* episode than reality.

Would our country ever be the same again? Had the world gone mad?

CHAPTER SEVEN

It seemed Devin never stood still. If he wasn't toiling at the brickyard or training with Reverend Patterson, he and Jesse worked on a 1955 Chevrolet sedan Devin had purchased from a Deland wrecking yard. Using Jesse's dad's pickup truck, they towed the Chevy to Cassadaga, where the car sat beside Grandma's garage on four bald tires.

My late grandfather had amassed a huge tool collection during his lifetime. The tools still occupied one portion of the garage. On a pegboard hung crescent wrenches, screwdrivers, socket wrenches, ball peen hammers, levels, wire cutters, tin snips, and adjustable clamps. Tool chests held electric drills, chisels, steel files, tape measures, and so forth. An electric motor, fitted with a circular wire brush, was useful for polishing metal; the motor was bolted to a tool bench. Shelves held coffee cans full of nuts and bolts, wood screws, sheet metal screws, and nails of varying sizes.

Friday nights, I'd often find Devin and Jesse out back, with Jesse's transistor radio blaring Roy Orbison or The Supremes. The hood of the Chevrolet was usually raised, and a utility light cast its glow into the car's cavernous engine compartment. With Chilton's repair manual always at hand, they removed parts, cleaned them with kerosene, and then returned the parts to their rightful places, using a screwdriver or wrench.

I'd never been interested in cars. Who cared how they worked, as long as they ran? But now, I liked watching Jesse and Devin tinker. Often shirtless, they'd lean against the Chevy's fender, staring at the engine, their hips touching, and their lean torsos on display. I'd think of the day at the spring when I'd watched them have sex, and my mouth would get sticky.

They're beautiful—both of them. Will I ever have a boyfriend so perfect?

In northeast Florida, in 1963, men didn't use deodorant, and I found both guys' body odors arousing: Devin's soured-milk scent, Jesse's musky aroma. I felt like a kid in a bakery, sniffing their flesh while my groin tingled.

Jesse told us his family had moved to Orange City from Jacksonville, after Jesse's dad lost his job there.

"He worked as caretaker at a wealthy family's estate. We lived in a furnished cottage on their property. It was nice, like living in a park. You wouldn't believe the money some folks have."

"Why'd he lose the job?" I asked.

"Booze," Jesse answered, shaking his head.

While watching Devin and Jesse work on the Chevy, I learned a slew of automotive terms: carburetor, brake shoe, lug nut, wheel bearing, spark plug, head gasket, and master cylinder. Jesse and Devin showed me how to fill battery cells with sterile water, how to drain the gas tank and clean it, how to replace wiper blades, headlamps, and dashboard bulbs.

The Chevy's paint was battleship gray and heavily oxidized. The car's chrome bumpers were pitted with rust, and its interior smelled like an old work boot. The cloth upholstery was split in several places, the headliner sagged, and neither the radio nor the clock worked because the battery was dead.

My grandma called it a "jalopy," but I loved the Chevy, despite its shabby appearance and inability to run. Sometimes, I'd sit behind the wheel and daydream about driving the Chevy to school, rather than riding the school bus. How cool would that be?

Devin spent his Saturdays with Rev. Patterson, observing her methods of speaking with the departed, watching her read tarot cards and palms. She performed these services at her private residence, a grand place by Cassadaga standards. A Queen Anne structure built in the late 1890s, the house featured a turret, multiple chimneys, scalloped siding, and a wraparound porch with cylindrical support columns. The house stood beside a small lake on her acreage, where Muscovy ducks waddled about the banks, searching for bugs.

"She has a special room for meeting clients," Devin told me. "You should see the furnishings: velvet drapes, a crystal chandelier, fancy wallpaper, Oriental rugs. The chairs and sofa are leather. The coffee table's as big as a door, and the fireplace mantle is marble; it looks like a temple in some history book."

Rev. Patterson employed a gardener, a red-haired half-wit named Rufus. He was dumb as a post, but looked like a J. C. Penney catalog model. His chin was prominent, his waist narrow, and his shoulders brushed doorjambs when he entered a room. Sometimes we saw him on the street in Cassadaga, and Devin would always greet Rufus. The two would shake hands, and then Rufus would babble nonsense. He always wore tight-fitting overalls, and if he sported an erection—which he often did—you could see the outline of his daunting member, a thing as big as a cucumber.

Once, after we encountered Rufus at the hardware

store, I told Devin of Grandma's remarks about Rev. Patterson and her omnivorous sex life.

Devin giggled and shook his head.

"She keeps Rufus busy."

"So, it's true?"

He nodded.

"What about you? Has she ever made a pass?"

Devin nodded again.

"What did you do?" I asked.

Devin raised a shoulder. "It's important I stay in her good graces. Sometimes I let her touch me, sometimes I touch her."

My jaw sagged and my eyes bugged. "Does Jesse know?"

He shook his head. "And don't repeat what I've told you."

His revelation bewildered me. How could a guy who screwed men also have sex with women? The thought of Devin in bed with Rev. Patterson made my skin crawl. She had to be forty at least; she was ancient. It didn't seem fair *she* could touch Devin, but I couldn't.

I shook my head.

Life's rules didn't make any sense, did they?

CHAPTER EIGHT

Fake left with your head, then shift the ball to your right hand. Drive to the goal and lay it up."
It was Christmas Eve. The weather was cool, but Devin's T-shirt was sweat-soaked; mine was too. School was out, the brickyard was closed, and the day was ours.

I followed Devin's instructions. Taking two steps as I drew near the goal, I leapt into the air, arm outstretched, the ball cradled in my hand. I launched the ball, and then it ricocheted off the backboard; it whizzed through the goal.

"Good one," Devin cried.

Since his arrival in August, we'd practiced most every weekday—during the hour preceding dinner—and I'd learned a lot. Now, my jump shot was accurate, my ball handling quicker, and I rarely missed a lay-up. My free-throw percentage was close to eighty-five. Devin had purchased a cotton net for the goal, and I liked the swishy sound the net made when the ball passed through it.

When Devin wasn't around, I practiced alone. I'd place a row of Grandma's dining room chairs on the driveway, spaced four feet apart. Then I'd dribble back and forth between them, zigzagging like a bee, for hours. At night, I'd practice under the glow from a gooseneck light fixture bolted to a corner of the garage. The fixture's bulb cast a cone of light, attracting moths and other fluttering insects.

I had grown two inches since Devin's arrival; now I was five-eight. Devin still had four inches on me, but my increased height made it harder for Devin to defend against me when we played one-on-one. I still could not beat him, of course, but his margins of victory had narrowed.

"Let's take a break," Devin said now. "I need a smoke."

We sat on the back steps. Devin puffed, while I stared at the mackerel sky, savoring Devin's body odor. His soured-milk scent had always excited me, and now my crotch stirred when I inhaled.

I glanced over at Devin. "Will you quit your job when you open shop?"

The previous week, Rev. Patterson had advised the Council of Mediums that Devin had served his apprenticeship with distinction. She wrote Rev. Hagermann, "The boy has a gift, and I want him to share it. I want his spirituality to flourish."

My grandma snorted when she heard about the letter. She told my mom, "It's not Devin's 'spirituality' she's cultivating, I'm sure."

Mom hissed. "Devin's just a boy. Surely you don't think—"

Grandma snorted again. "Wise up, Brenda. Grace Patterson can't be trusted around *any* male who's reached puberty. And Devin's been in prison; he's not innocent."

Three days before, over Grandma's objection, the council had voted. They would allow Devin to open a practice in Cassadaga. Their approval had never been in doubt, really, not after Devin performed a "sitting" with Rev. Gloria Hagermann herself, an event observed by dozens of folks, including me and several council members, at Colby Memorial Temple. Devin had communicated with Rev. Hagermann's deceased daughter Helen, the girl murdered twenty-five years before.

During the sitting, Devin and Rev. Hagermann sat in ladderback chairs, facing each other. A cotton dress, once belonging to Helen Hagermann, rested in Devin's lap. With his head bowed and his eyes closed, Devin told Rev. Hagermann, "Helen wants you to know she's fine. In the spirit world, she's healthy and happy, but she misses her house cat, Tippy."

Rev. Hagermann's eyebrows arched. She rearranged herself in her chair while Devin continued.

"Helen wonders if you kept the rhinestone necklace she bought you at the dime store in Daytona Beach. It was your thirty-sixth birthday gift, remember?"

Rev. Hagermann dipped her chin and blinked. The temple was silent as a tomb.

"She says her favorite books, as a girl, were her Nancy Drew mysteries. She wants to know if you've kept them?"

Rev. Hagermann looked up at Devin, her eyes watering. "Tell her I said, 'No. I'm sorry but I gave them to the public library. They made me sad whenever I looked at them.'"

Devin worked his jaw from side to side. Then he nodded. "She says, 'It's all right, Mama. I understand; I don't want you to be sad.'"

At that point, Rev. Hagermann buried her face in her hands and wept like a child. Her shoulders shook like palm fronds in a stiff breeze.

Grace Patterson looked at my grandma and raised her eyebrows. When I glanced at Grandma, *her* eyebrows were gathered.

There in the temple, Grandma shook her head. She told my mom, "I've never seen anything like this. I still say something's fishy."

Now, on Grandma's steps, Devin stubbed out his cigarette in the coffee can he kept there. He said, "I'll keep my job awhile; I'll perform sittings on weekends and evenings until business picks up. Then I'll quit the brickyard."

On Christmas Day, in the afternoon, I shot baskets with a new ball Devin had given me, an official NCAA model, made of leather. It produced pleasant, thunking sounds when I dribbled on the driveway. I wore a Los Angeles Lakers jersey Mom had placed under the tree: a blue-and-white, rayon beauty with Jerry West's name and the number 44 on the back.

The sky was overcast, and a cool wind blew from the east. The wind stirred fronds on a Sabal palm in my grandma's backyard, making rustling noises. Out front, a car engine hummed. A door slammed, a neighbor's dog barked, and when I rounded the corner of Grandma's house, I saw Jesse and Devin drive off in Jesse's dad's pickup truck. Smoke spewed from the truck's tailpipe.

Clutching the ball to my chest, I chewed my lips. I worked the toe of my sneaker into the grass while I stared down the road.

Where were they going? What would they do?

I was very much in love with Devin, and terribly jealous of Jesse.

Most Saturday nights, Devin and Jesse would ride the bus to Daytona Beach; they'd see a movie or shoot pool. Then they'd split the cost of a cheap motel room. Sunday, they'd return by bus.

I had once asked Devin if the two of them slept in the same bed when they stayed in Daytona.

He chuckled in response.

"What do *you* think, Ty?"

Now, just in time for Christmas dinner, Devin returned home. He sat across from me at the dining room table, with candlelight reflecting in his eyes. My gaze fell upon a signet ring he wore on his left hand, a jewelry item I'd never seen before. I opened my mouth to ask Devin about it, but before I could speak, he looked up from his plate. His gaze met mine, and he shook his head, subtly.

Later that evening, in Devin's room, we sat on his bed, and then he raised his left hand. Light from the ceiling fixture reflected in three letters engraved on the ring's plateau—"JSA," in fancy script. The tattoos on Devin's fingers looked shabby compared to the ring's monogram.

"I gave Jesse one with *my* initials on it," Devin said.

My spirits sank like a stone flung into a pond. Jesse and Devin were in love, weren't they? They shared a private universe now, one I'd never be part of. Devin cared nothing for me, did he?

My eyes itched, and my nose clogged. I struck my hands between my knees. Then my face crumpled, and I wept like a baby.

Devin put his arm about my shoulders.

"Ty, don't worry. Your time will come."

"When?"

"Sooner than you think," was Devin's reply.

CHAPTER NINE

On a blustery Wednesday night, in late March, I lay in my bed, arms folded behind my head, my gaze fixed on the ceiling. The moon kept emerging and disappearing, while clouds skated across the inky sky. Wind gusts rattled my windows. Outside the window, branches of a longleaf pine tossed about, its needles fluttering. Grandma's oil-burning furnace wasn't too effective; the room was chilly, and I shivered under my blanket. I rubbed one foot against the other, to keep both warm.

Go to sleep, Tyler.

I closed my eyes. Then I tried a relaxation technique Devin had told me recently about, one he'd learned in prison.

"It always helps me snooze, when I feel keyed up."

I drew a breath, held it ten seconds, and then exhaled. I drew another breath, held it ten seconds, and then exhaled. I kept this up for a couple of minutes, and it did relax me some. But then something curious happened.

A vision entered my head, quite vivid. I felt as if my conscious mind had departed my body. In my vision, I sat at my desk in English class, where afternoon sunlight slanted in through the western windows. I wore a collared shirt, blue jeans, and my basketball sneakers—the same outfit I'd worn to school, two days before. An open textbook lay before me on my desk return. I read aloud from Chaucer's *Canterbury Tales*, just as I had the day before yesterday. But now my viewpoint moved about the room, independent of my body, like a film camera on a crane. I saw everyone present, saw whatever they did. Moreover, I knew exactly what thoughts dwelt in each person's head: my teacher, Mrs. Calhoun; our intern teacher, a Miss Pritchard, visiting from Florida State University; and all my classmates.

Mrs. Calhoun was not concentrating on the Chaucer I read. Instead, she pondered a recipe for three-bean chili she would prepare that evening. A girl seated two rows behind me, Angela Chastain, twisted a lock of hair around her finger. She thought about her last date, and how her boyfriend had touched her breasts when they'd tongue-kissed in his car.

A guy named Butch DeLay—scion of a notorious Deland redneck family and one of the toughest kids in the sophomore class—chewed a filthy hangnail. He recalled his fistfight, occurring two days before, with a senior who'd outweighed Butch by forty pounds. Butch's left eye was swollen shut and purple, his lower lip was puffy, and he picked at a scab on his cheek. But I'd passed Butch's adversary in the school hallway that morning. He looked even worse than Butch: bruised and scabby and limping like he'd been in a car accident.

My gaze fell upon Eric Rupp, a slender, sandy-haired boy with blue-green eyes, and a riot of freckles dancing across his turned-up nose. We knew each other by name, but we'd never hung out together. In Mrs. Calhoun's class, he sat one row behind me and to the right, so under normal circumstances I would not have seen what Eric did as I read to the classroom. But now I saw everything: Eric's gaze was fixed upon me. He studied my hair, my neck and shoulder, and my arm. He watched my knee flop from side to side—a nervous tic of mine—while my voice droned away.

Eric's mind wasn't on Chaucer either. Instead he daydreamed. In his imagination, he and I occupied a bedroom with a Red Sox baseball pennant hung on the wall. Eric sat on the edge of a double bed while I stood before him, shirtless. Sunlight entered the bedroom, reflecting off a desk lamp. Eric worked open the button at the waist of my jeans; his knuckles dug into my belly, while I flexed my toes. Eric parted the flaps of my jeans. Then he shucked the jeans to my knees.

I placed a hand on the back of Eric's neck, and then—

A wind gust rattled my bedroom window. I jerked in surprise, and then my eyelids fluttered open. Glancing here and there, I wasn't sure where I was at first. Beneath my sheet and blanket, the pouch of my underwear felt damp and sticky. My armpits were moist, and beads of sweat decorated my forehead.

What was going on? What had just happened?

Had I dreamt?

Or was it possible I had just taken a psychic journey? Could I sometimes read other persons' thoughts?

And what of Eric Rupp? Had that been *his* sexual fantasy or mine?

I scratched my belly and shifted my shoulders.

Maybe spirituality isn't "bunk" after all.

"Transcendental Meditation," Devin said. "Ever heard of it?"

The previous night's storm had left Grandma's lawn strewn with pine branches and palm fronds. Now, Devin and I gathered them into a wheelbarrow. We would take them out back, stack them, and set them afire, using kerosene. A cold front had followed the storm, and the sky was bright, the sun as shiny as a new quarter. The afternoon air smelled of sodden pine bark and damp clay. Devin wore his brickyard outfit; I wore an old pair of jeans and a T-shirt too stained to wear to school.

I had just told Devin about the previous night's experience in my bedroom, though I kept details of Eric Rupp's reverie to myself.

Devin said, "Some folks don't believe in TM, but I do. The breathing technique helps your mind relax. Sometimes, you leave the physical world behind, and then you experience a different type of consciousness. Understand?"

I nodded, but I wasn't sure I believed what Devin had just said. The whole thing sounded like... voodoo bullshit.

I said, "Was I reading my teacher's thoughts? Or did my imagination make me think I could?"

Devin dropped an armload of palm fronds into the wheelbarrow. Then he looked at me.

"Here's how to find out: tomorrow, ask your teacher how her chili tasted on Tuesday."

Devin winked at me like a conspirator.

I lowered my gaze and patted my chin with my fingertips. Was it possible I possessed a "gift" myself? If so, how should I use it?

Mrs. Calhoun wouldn't stop staring while I took my Friday vocabulary test. Earlier, before class had started, when I asked about her chili, a crease formed between her eyebrows. She raised her upper lip, as though she'd just viewed something spectral.

"It was quite good, thank you, Tyler," was all she

managed to say, and I knew I'd startled the bejeezus out of her.

I walked to my desk with a smile playing on my lips. *It's not bullshit after all. The breathing exercise works.*

Moments later, when Eric Rupp passed by my desk, I looked at his crimson mouth. I felt a stirring in my pants when I thought of kissing him.

He's probably yours if you want him, Tyler.
Do you?

Early on a Friday evening, as the sun dipped below the western tree line and bats flitted about, Jesse and I watched Devin attach cables to posts on the Chevrolet's new battery, using a socket wrench. After lowering the hood and securing the latch, he looked at Jesse, then me.

"Well," he said, "I guess it's time."

Jesse and Devin both wore their filthy brickyard clothing; they smelled of sweat. I wore my school clothes. I climbed into the backseat. Then Devin sat behind the wheel, with Jesse next to him on the passenger side. The dome light's glow illuminated the Chevy's new headliner; it was taut as a drumhead. I ran my hand over the soft upholstery; every split in the cloth had been repaired. The chrome door handles and window cranks gleamed, the carpets smelled of shampoo, and the wood trim on the dashboard shone. Now that the battery had been connected, the clock's second hand skipped like a kid playing hopscotch.

Devin placed the key in the ignition; he pumped the gas pedal twice and looked at Jesse.

"You ready?"

Jesse bobbed his chin.

I held my breath while Devin twisted the key. Would

the car really come to life?

The starter clicked and the engine sputtered, but did not catch.

Devin looked at Jesse and cursed.

"Relax," Jesse said. "Try again."

Devin pumped the gas pedal; he grimaced when twisting the key. The starter clicked, the engine coughed, and this time the motor turned over. *Chug-chug. Rum-m-m-m.* My scalp prickled when Devin switched on the headlights and the Chevy's dashboard instruments illuminated. When Jesse twisted a knob on the radio, Elvis Presley's voice wafted from a speaker.

A chill ran up my spine. The Chevy was a mechanical Lazarus, wasn't it? Devin's and Jesse's labors had resurrected it from automotive death.

Unbelievable.

We all hooted and stamped our feet. Jesse grabbed Devin by the neck; he planted a kiss on Devin's cheek. Then the two of them stared at each other for a long moment, while Devin grinned and batted his eyelashes.

I broke the silence. "Change the radio station; find some Beatles. Then let's drive someplace."

They both turned and looked at me. Devin drew a breath and lowered his gaze.

"Ty," he said, "we'll give you a ride later, but right now..."

"What?"

Devin returned his gaze to me.

"Jesse and I need to be alone. You understand, don't you?"

I felt like I'd stepped off a cliff. My eyes watered as I left the car. Why was life so unfair? Why must *I* be excluded from this glorious moment? Would Devin and Jesse always treat me like a punk?

After shifting into reverse, Devin backed the Chevy

toward the street. The engine purred, and the headlights cast cones of light. I stood on the driveway with my arms folded across my chest, watching the Chevy's taillights fade.

A tear rolled down my cheek.

CHAPTER TEN

My grandma stood at her living room window, holding a curtain aside and shaking her head. A news reporter and a press photographer stood on the sidewalk before her house, looking our way.

"Will they never go away?" she said to no one in particular.

Cassadaga had turned into a hubbub in recent days, for reasons Grandma had explained to me, after her conversation with Rev. Gloria Hagermann.

Days before, a Duval County sheriff's detective had sought Rev. Hagermann's assistance. He was investigating the kidnapping of one Julia Ball, a ten-year-old girl from a wealthy Jacksonville family, folks related to the DuPonts. A ransom note had been left in Julia's bedroom, but the kidnappers had not made contact with the family since then.

The detective said the child had been missing two weeks.

"I've run out of leads," the detective told Rev. Hagermann. "The trail's cold."

He produced a pair of Julia's unwashed panties.

Rev. Hagermann tried her best, but in the end, she could not help. Exasperated, she mentioned Devin.

Perhaps, she said, he could be of assistance.

The detective brought Devin home from the brickyard. After Devin showered and dressed in clean clothes, the two of them occupied Devin's room more than two hours, with the door closed.

"It wasn't easy," Devin told us at the dinner table, afterward. "The child died a violent death. Her spirit's agitated; she resists contact with the living. So, it took awhile, but I finally got her to speak, to describe the location of her body."

Grandma, my mom, and I listened while untouched food cooled on our plates.

"It's a sawmill," Devin said, "one not operating anymore. There's a broken-down truck on the property with a company's name on it. The girl spelled it out for me."

Next morning, while we breakfasted at Grandma's kitchen table, Devin received a call from the sheriff's detective. Julia Ball's body had been found near Palatka, Florida, at the abandoned premises of Putnam Lumber Company. The child had been strangled, and then left beneath a canvas tarp. Wild creatures, likely feral dogs, had discovered her remains; they tore her apart, and now she was barely recognizable.

A Jacksonville television station broke the news. When Devin returned from work that evening, a phalanx of reporters and photographers converged upon him before Grandma's house. Questions were shouted while flashbulbs popped. Devin squinted into the brightness of a TV cameraman's light, answering questions, looking handsome and composed, despite his sweat-stained T-shirt, filthy jeans, and work boots.

Now, our phone wouldn't stop ringing. Newspapers from Atlanta, Dallas, Chicago, and New York called to interview Devin. A film crew from NBC's affiliate station in Miami came to Cassadaga, also to interview Devin, but more in depth. The next night, we all watched on a neighbor's television while Chet Huntley described the kidnapping and murder of Julia Ball. Huntley spoke of Devin's assistance in locating her body while Devin's image appeared on the flickering, black-and-white screen. Devin wore his Banlon shirt, and the glow from TV camera spotlights reflected in his carefully styled hair. His voice sounded just like it did at home.

"We're indebted to him," the detective said of Devin, during the NBC broadcast. "Without his help we'd never have found the girl."

The press people weren't the only folks calling Grandma's house. Devin received calls from police officials and private detectives, from persons who'd lost loved ones and wished to speak with them, and from mediums throughout the country who wished to refer business to Devin. Our telephone shared a party line with three other households, and they complained so much my grandma had our number converted to a private line, at Devin's expense.

"If this keeps up," she told Devin, "you'll have to purchase a second line."

Already, Devin pondered quitting his job.

"It doesn't pay well," he said at the dinner table. "Doing sittings, I'd earn more in a day than I would in two weeks at the brickyard."

My grandma fingered her pearls. "Where would you practice?"

Devin rearranged himself in his chair and cleared his throat. "Grace Patterson's offered me use of her home. I'll pay her something each time I'm there."

Grandma looked at my mom and rolled her eyes.

CHAPTER ELEVEN

On a Friday afternoon in mid-April, I boarded Eric Rupp's school bus, toting an overnight bag. I would spend the night at his home in Deland.

I didn't care much about baseball. But during the past few weeks, I'd studied Red Sox statistics in the 1964 *Street & Smith's Baseball Annual*, and I'd learned enough to convince Eric I was a fan. I chose the Red Sox left fielder, Carl Yastrzemski, as my favorite player. Then I memorized his personal data: *throws right, bats left, his 1963 batting average was .321, he made the 1963 American League All Stars, hit 14 homers, had 68 RBIs.*

A few days before, I had sidled up to Eric in the hallway at school. I asked him, "Do you think Boston will win today's opener against the Yankees?"

Posing the question to Eric was like opening a water spigot. He *spewed* statistics: both teams' win-loss records in 1963, the names of opening day pitchers for the Yanks and Red Sox, the teams' likely batting lineups, and so forth.

I countered with Yastrzemski's numbers while Eric listened, bobbing his chin. He said, "Did you know Yaz placed tenth in the American League's MVP race last year?"

I didn't, but said I did anyway.

We talked about Boston's upcoming game on Saturday, against Chicago. When I told Eric we didn't have a TV at my home, that I'd listen to the game on the radio, he looked at me like I lived in Paraguay.

"Come to my house," he said. "We'll watch it together."

Okay, Tyler, finesse this...

Shoving my hands into my hip pockets, I looked at my shoes and let out my breath.

"I'd love to," I said, "but I can't."

Eric asked why.

"I won't have transportation. My mom works Saturdays, and she'll take our car to Daytona Beach. My grandma doesn't drive."

Eric kept his gaze low while he stubbed the hallway concrete with his sneaker toe.

"Spend the night at my house Friday," he said. "You can ride the bus home with me."

I closed my eyelids.

Yeah, that's perfect.

Now, on the bus, Eric and I shared a seat. Our hips, knees, and elbows touched. Eric sat next to the open window. Air rushing into the bus fluttered his sandy hair; the breeze blew his bangs into his blue-green eyes. I kept glancing at the fuzz on his upper lip, wondering how would it feel if I kissed him? Up close, his eyes had a glittery appearance. His voice had the rasp of a guy in his mid-teens; it sometimes cracked into falsetto when he spoke, and the freckles on his nose gave his face a boyish look. But the bulge in his crotch wasn't childlike at all.

Eric's home was two-storied, with a screened front porch and a live oak shading the yard. He produced a house key from beneath a flowerpot on the porch. "My folks run a dry cleaning business," he said. "They won't be home 'til six."

Eric's bedroom looked exactly as it had in my vision—the one I'd experienced weeks before: double bed, Red Sox pennant, desk, and chair, jute rug. A triangular "Yield" sign Eric had stolen from a road shoulder hung on a wall. Afternoon sunlight entered through a pair of double-hung windows. Eric kept his baseball card collection in a shoebox. After he brought out the box, he motioned me to sit beside him on his bed. Again, our hips and knees and shoulders touched. My pulse quickened while Eric chattered away and his breath swept my forearm. Each time he handed me a card, our wrists or fingers made contact, and my belly fluttered.

I smelled Eric's hair and skin; their scents made my pulse quicken.

We looked at cards for half an hour or so. Then Eric placed the shoebox on his nightstand. He flopped onto his back, next to me on the mattress. After folding his arms behind his head, he stared at the ceiling and moistened his lips. His feet rested on the jute rug. The hem of Eric's T-shirt had lifted, and now I stared at his belly button and the waistband of his underwear.

Tyler, I think this may be an invitation...

I followed Eric's lead, lying beside him and staring at the ceiling, close enough so our hips and shoulders touched. We lay there in silence a minute or so, our chests rising and falling. Then I moved my hand, so my knuckles met Eric's hipbone.

Eric turned his face toward mine. After swallowing, he pointed to my zipper.

"Have you ever measured yourself when you're stiff?"

I looked into Eric's eyes. "Not in a while. How about you?"

"It's been a few months."

My pulse pounded in my temples, and my voice cracked when I spoke.

"Got a ruler?" I asked.

CHAPTER TWELVE

I rarely entered my grandma's bedroom, as nothing in there interested me. But on a rainy afternoon in May, my writing pen went dry while I worked on a book report for Mrs. Calhoun. ("William Golding's book, *Lord of the Flies*, is an allegorical novel discussing how any culture created by man is doomed to failure.") Grandma's rolltop desk, crafted from golden oak, was a massive thing with dozens of cubbyholes. She kept a fistful of ballpoint pens in the pencil drawer, bound together with a rubber band, and now I helped myself to one.

Outside, lightning flickered and a thunderclap shook the house.

My gaze traveled about the room. Grandma's sleigh bed could have slept four adults. The Oriental rug was worn to its weft in places. A photographic portrait of my grandfather, in his WWI uniform, hung above a highboy dresser with a marble top. I stepped before Grandma's full-length dressing mirror, and then I studied my reflection. I'd grown another two inches since Christmas, and now the cuffs of my jeans rode above my ankles. I was five-foot-ten, my shoulders had broadened, and my biceps and chest muscles bulged beneath my T-shirt.

Not bad, Buckspan.

I stepped to a bookcase as tall as me; it held scores of books: treatises on the spiritual world, biographies, romance novels, and, of course, Grandma's diaries, dozens of volumes in varying sizes, some paperbacked, others bound in leather, all with dates inscribed on their spines, the earliest being 1907.

I opened a dusty volume from the years 1917 and 1918, admiring Grandma's precise penmanship; it slanted a bit to the right:

Received a letter from Elmer today. His unit is entrenched in Flanders. He suffers from dysentery and a gum disorder the soldiers call "trench mouth." He says the food is terrible, the weather worse. How he misses Florida's tropical climate.

I closed the book and returned it to its rightful place, shaking my head. Someday would *I* own this bookcase? Would the flimsy notebooks I'd used to record events of my days someday occupy these shelves? And what would become of Grandma's collection when she passed away?

Spring water beaded on Eric Rupp's shoulders. The drops looked like gemstones, reflecting sunlight. I stood behind Eric, waist-deep in the spring, my arms wrapped about his chest, my hips pressed to his buttocks. We had just made love on a bedsheet; it lay crumpled on the shore. June's heat had made our sex a sweaty, sticky affair, but now the spring cooled our flesh.

I listened to water drip, to Eric's soft breathing. My chin rested against the back of his neck, and I buried the tip of my nose in his damp hair.

Since my first visit to Eric's home, we had made love

any number of places: his house, my grandma's, the spring, and even the backseat of the Chevrolet, one afternoon when a thunderstorm raged. I'd never felt so close to someone; I had touched every part of Eric's body. His dad owned a tent and sleeping bags. On weekends, we'd often camp by the spring's edge. We had constructed a fire pit, girding its walls with chunks of lime rock, and thereafter we always burned pine limbs during our evenings there, listening to sap crackle and hiss, watching sparks rise into the night sky.

"Will it always be like this?" Eric asked me one evening.

We lay side by side in his tent. The mildewed smell of the canvas made my nose crinkle. Beyond the tent flaps, a campfire smoldered. I lay on my back with my gaze fixed on the canvas overhead.

"I hope so," I said.

Shifting his weight, Eric asked me, "Are you and I queers?"

I cleared my throat. "I suppose," I said.

Eric turned toward me; he crooked an elbow and propped his head against his hand. "Does it scare you, being... different?"

"A little. We'll have to be careful, always."

After draping his arm across my belly, Eric laid his cheek against my sternum. "I think I'm in love with you, Tyler. Is that okay?"

My windpipe flexed, and then my eyes watered.

Holy crap.

"Of course it is," I whispered.

CHAPTER THIRTEEN

The second week of June arrived, and school let out for summer. In a month, I'd turn sixteen; I could qualify for a driver's license. With Mom's permission, Devin drove me to the DMV office in Deland, where I earned a learner's permit, and thereafter Devin gave me lessons whenever time permitted.

But Devin had little free time.

Since opening his practice in Rev. Patterson's home, he'd been deluged with business. People came from as far away as Vermont and Arizona for sittings, and police detectives frequently contacted Devin about their cold cases. Even the wife of Florida's governor bought an hour of Devin's time.

"She wanted to speak with her mother, who'd passed six years ago," Devin told my mom and me, after the sitting.

When I asked Devin how much he charged his clients, he said, "That's a 'none-ya,' Ty."

"A *what*?"

"It's none of your business."

But Devin, I figured, must be earning substantial sums from sittings he conducted at Grace Patterson's home. He'd bought himself a new wardrobe from the best department store in Orlando: a dozen collared dress shirts, several neckties, expensive slacks, and two wool business suits: one gray, the other dark blue with pinstripes. He bought a half dozen pairs of leather shoes, some lace-ups, others slip-ons, one pair two-toned. He acquired a camel's hair sports jacket with oval patches on the elbows.

Devin purchased clothes for Jesse too. On Saturday nights, they'd both dress up like dandies. They styled their hair just so, with Brylcreem. Then they took the Chevy to Daytona Beach or St. Augustine, while I sat in my bedroom and sulked, feeling jealous of Jesse and the attention Devin gave him.

Devin bought me things as well: a new backboard and basketball goal, a silver identification bracelet with my initials monogrammed on the plate, and a gleaming English racer bicycle with caliper brakes and skinny tires. Devin slipped me cash from time to time, as well—five or ten dollars a pop. Sometimes, Eric and I would ride the bus to Daytona Beach, and I'd pay for dinner and a movie. In the darkness of the theater, Eric would hold my hand when we felt sure no one could see.

As much as I cared for Eric, and as good as our sex was, I was still crazy in love with Devin. At the dinner table, I couldn't keep my eyes off him. He'd found a good barber in Deland who styled Devin's hair just like the TV star Ed Burns on the series *77 Sunset Strip*. With his fancy new clothes and recent notoriety, Devin appealed more than ever to me.

We still played basketball, Devin and I. Not as much as before, but two or three times per week, we'd go at it.

"You're getting better," he told me one evening, when we played one-on-one and he barely beat me. "You should try out for your school's team this fall."

Devin paid for installation of an extension phone in his bedroom. Evenings, it rang frequently. If I were in my room, I'd often hear Devin converse behind his closed door, with whom I didn't know. But one night, when I lifted the downstairs receiver to call Eric, Devin already occupied the line.

"I can't," he said. "I already have plans."

"With whom?" a woman said.

"A friend is all. Don't be jealous."

"I *am* jealous. Tell your friend you're canceling. Spend Saturday night with me instead."

"I can't, I—"

"You can't or you won't?"

"Honey, don't get mad."

I crinkled my forehead while returning the receiver to its hook.

Who was Devin talking to?

On a weekday in July, just before my birthday, I joined my mom when she drove to work. I brought a towel and bathing trunks, a book to read as well, and I spent the day at the beach. I swam in the ocean and walked along the shore, daydreaming about Devin and about Eric Rupp too.

Eric's family vacationed in North Carolina at the time.

I thought of trying out for my high school's basketball team next season, as Devin had suggested. Could I make the cut? Basketball was a big deal at our school; the players were like celebrities. But so many guys at our school were bigger and faster than me. Was I kidding myself, thinking I might one day wear a uniform?

While I walked, I savored the roll of the waves and the smacking sound they made when they broke on the sand. The air smelled briny and fresh. Flocks of birds stood here and there: laughing gulls, sandwich terns, and herring gulls. They scattered at my approach, skipping on their spindly legs and crying at my intrusion. I found a piece of driftwood—a crooked thing as long as my leg, and skinny as broom handle—and then I carried it like a staff, poking the sand as I strode along and pondered my circumstances.

I still loved Devin; I fantasized about him in my bed at night, sometimes touching myself. But I knew he belonged to Jesse. For over nine months, they'd been boyfriends, and I didn't see how that would change. I'd never kiss Devin's lips or feel him inside me, I figured. I'd never fall asleep in Devin's arms, would I?

And what of Eric? At least twice a week, we made love, and the sex was awfully good. By now, each of us knew what the other liked. Our sessions often lasted ninety minutes or more; they were sensual and sweaty, but still...

Eric wasn't the brightest of boys. Aside from *Sporting News* and *Street & Smith's Baseball Annual*, he read only what was required of him at school. His grades were average, his interests limited to baseball, TV, and sex.

A touring company from New York performed the musical *West Side Story* at a Daytona Beach auditorium, and I bought tickets for Eric and me. On a Friday night, we took a bus to the east coast and attended the show. I enjoyed myself thoroughly – I especially liked the choreography—but Eric fell asleep before the first act ended.

I liked my studies at school. My grades were excellent, and I planned to attend the University of Florida in Gainesville, after graduating from high school. How would Eric fit into that picture? If we lived in separate towns, would our relationship wither and die like a houseplant someone had failed to water?

I thought about my mom. In recent months, she'd been cranky and constantly complaining about her work.

She was tired at the end of the day, she said. She detested women who patronized her shop and their endless gossip.

"I'm sick of smelling perm chemicals and nail polish. I'm tired of listening to hair dryers hum."

Evenings, she'd soak her feet in a shallow pan filled with Epsom salt solution. The pan would vibrate after she plugged it into a wall socket, and she'd sit there with her eyes closed, her lips pursed.

Mom and my grandma often quarreled over nonsense: house cleaning duties, what we'd eat for dinner, or which programs we listened to on the radio. They were like two scissor blades, constantly scraping against each other. More than once, I heard them squabble over Devin's continued presence in Grandma's house.

"He earns a good living now," Grandma said. "Why can't he find a place of his own?"

"He needs a stable home," Mom said. "And look how Tyler's blossomed since Devin came to town."

Now, in Daytona, as 5:00 p.m. drew near, my nose and cheeks burned. The bottoms of my feet hurt from walking on hot sand. I showered at a bathing pavilion, changed into my street clothes. Then I strolled toward Mom's shop. Heat shimmered off the sidewalk and asphalt roadbed. I passed few people; the weather was just too hot for most folks.

After turning a corner, I saw my mom conversing with a red-haired, slender woman in a waitress uniform, someone I didn't recognize. They stood beneath a canvas awning; it shaded the beauty parlor's plate-glass window. Both smoked cigarettes. When Mom noticed my approach, she dropped her butt to the sidewalk, and then ground it out with her shoe toe.

Mom said something to her companion, while both women looked in my direction. Then, before I came within earshot, the red-haired woman climbed into a battered Ford Comet with an Ormond Beach tag on its front bumper. She drove off, with her tailpipe spewing smoke.

"Who was that?" I asked Mom.

She shrugged.

"Just a customer," she said.

On July 22, 1964—my sixteenth birthday—my mother took the day off. She drove me to Deland, to the DMV office, where I took my road test in her Dodge Dart. A uniformed officer, a taciturn fellow with a beer gut and a bald spot, sat in the passenger seat, watching me adjust mirrors.

"Whenever you're ready," he said, "start the engine, shift into reverse, and back out of the space."

Thirty minutes later, after my flawless parallel parking performance, a woman took my photo and I left the DMV, license in hand, a grin on my face. My mom kissed my cheek. She bought us cheeseburgers, fries, and soft drinks at a fast food place. Then, after we ate, she let me drive us back to Cassadaga. Clutching the steering wheel, I grinned as we flew past palmetto-and-pine forests. Suddenly, I felt much older, and more mature.

I wasn't a boy anymore, was I?

CHAPTER FOURTEEN

At my grandmother's dinner table, in mid-August, Devin looked at me, then my mom and Grandma. He told us, "I married Grace Patterson yesterday, at the courthouse in Deland."

I dropped my fork while blood drained from my head. My jaw quivered, and my hands shook.

Devin was married? How could it be? And what could be worse? He may as well have told us he'd been diagnosed with a terminal illness.

My mother beamed at Devin. "Honey, that's wonderful news. I hope you'll be happy."

Grandma clutched her pearls and glared at Devin. "How old is Grace, early forties?"

Devin nodded.

Grandma looked at me, then my mom.

"It's crazy," she said.

Looking back at Devin, Grandma told him, "She's old enough to be your mother."

Devin rearranged himself in his chair. He told Grandma, "Age isn't important; not when you're truly in love."

Mom placed her hand on Devin's forearm.

"Where will you live, at Rev. Patterson's?"

Devin nodded.

Mom said, "From the outside, it looks lovely. I can't wait to see the interior."

Devin said, "We'll have everyone for supper, real soon."

My voice cracked when I spoke.

"Devin?"

He looked at me with his eyebrows arched.

"Have you told Jesse?"

Hours after Devin's announcement, I lay in my darkened bedroom, staring at the ceiling while tears spilled from the corners of my eyes. For a year, Devin had dwelt in our home; he'd been my confidant, buddy, lust object, and teacher. Now, he would *leave* me for Grace Patterson? It didn't make sense. Why was life so unfair?

A knock sounded at my door.

"Ty, may I come in?"

Devin sat on the edge of my bed, wearing briefs and nothing else. I smelled his skin, and I thought of the first day he'd come to Cassadaga. The memory made my heart ache. How would I endure Devin's departure?

A slice of moonlight entered the room, enough so I saw the line of hair descending from Devin's bellybutton. Morose as I was, I felt a stirring in my groin, looking at his trail.

Devin laid a hand on my thigh and squeezed. "I know you're surprised and disappointed, but it's for the best."

"How could that be? You love Jesse, and he loves you."

"True. But some things are more important than love."

"Such as?"

"Money, for one thing. Building a future's another. Jesse will never leave that brickyard, Tyler; I guarantee it."

I rubbed the tip of my nose with a knuckle and sniffled.

"Do you love Rev. Patterson?"

Devin shrugged. "She's good to me."

"Will I still see you? Can we play basketball and swim at the spring?"

He nodded. "I'll only be blocks away."

Under the covers, I shifted my hips.

"When will you tell Jesse?"

Devin raised his shoulders.

"Does Rev. Patterson know?"

"What?"

"About you and Jesse? Does she know he's your boyfriend?"

Devin shook his head. "That's the sort of thing men keep to themselves. Understand?"

I said yes, but truthfully I *didn't* understand.

Not any of it.

On Labor Day morning, I lay on the glider sofa, on Grandma's front porch. I stared at the beadboard ceiling and cobwebs festooning it. Mom and my grandma had driven to Jacksonville, where several department stores held holiday sales, so I was alone. A mockingbird tootled in Grandma's gardenia bush. Dew glistened in her Bahia lawn.

I shifted my hips and blinked. What would I do with my day?

Then a familiar chug sounded. I rose to a sitting position, just as Devin pulled to the curb in the Chevrolet.

He'd moved from Grandma's house the week before, and I had not seen him since.

When he sat beside me on the glider, I smelled his cologne. He wore a sports jacket, a Banlon shirt, dress slacks, and leather slip-ons. His hair gleamed, and my heart fluttered at the sight of his lean physique.

He said, "I guess school starts tomorrow?"

I nodded.

After reaching inside his jacket, Devin produced an envelope. "Something for you."

Inside the envelope, I found the Chevrolet's certificate of title.

Devin pointed to his signature on the backside.

"Now you won't have to ride the school bus."

My jaw slacked while I studied the document. Then I looked at Devin.

"I don't understand. What'll you drive?"

"Grace bought me a Buick convertible. It's a wedding gift."

I nodded. Fingering the edge of the certificate, I studied Florida's Great Seal: an Indian woman scattering blossoms, a Sabal palm, a brilliant sun, and a double-masted sailing vessel.

What could I say?

I looked up at Devin.

"What about Jesse? Isn't it his car too?"

Devin shook his head. "I bought it myself and paid for all the parts. He only helped with repairs."

I licked my lips. "What did he say when you told him you were married?"

After looking away, Devin rubbed his knees with his palms. "I haven't told him yet; he thinks I'm Grace's tenant, nothing more."

I started. "When *will* you tell him?"

Devin didn't answer. Instead, he gave me the Chevy's ignition and trunk keys; they dangled from a flimsy chain.

"Give me a ride home, will you, Ty?"

CHAPTER FIFTEEN

Two weeks after fall semester began, I leaned against the Chevy's fender in my school's parking lot, waiting for Eric. Cumulus clouds cruised across a brilliant Florida sky, while a northeast wind stirred branches of a nearby live oak. My route to and from school passed Eric's house. Each day, I'd pick him up in the morning; then I'd drop him off in the afternoon. Often, after school let out for the day, we'd leave the County Road on our way home. We'd park behind an abandoned warehouse, and then we'd make love in the Chevy's backseat.

It was often warm inside the car in September's heat. We'd both sweat, and our skins smacked, wherever we made contact. Our sex was sticky and smelly, but I found each session intensely erotic.

Now, in the parking lot, Eric approached with a notebook and text under his arm. The breeze tossed his sandy hair, and his untied shoelace flipped here and there. My belly fluttered when I looked at him. Eric had grown taller, more muscular since we'd become lovers. He was no longer a boy, and the thought of lowering his zipper, minutes from now, quickened my pulse. I felt a stirring in my briefs, but when Eric drew near he did not smile as he normally might. His forehead crinkled, and one corner of his mouth turned down.

"Something wrong?" I asked.

He raised his eyebrows. "You haven't heard?"

"What?"

"About Devin's friend, Jesse?"

I shook my head.

Eric looked at something over my shoulder. Shifting his weight from one leg to the other, he worked his jaw from side to side.

"Tell me," I said.

Eric drew a breath and then his gaze met mine.

"Jesse killed himself this morning. He drove his dad's pickup into the woods. Then he stuck a shotgun in his mouth and blew his brains out."

What?

My knees quivered while my vision lost focus. I turned and placed my hands on the Chevy's trunk.

Jesse was dead? How could it be?

Eric laid a hand on my shoulder and squeezed. "I'm sorry, Tyler. I know Jesse and Devin were best friends."

My stomach churned, and I couldn't help myself: I puked, three or four times. My vomit glistened on the Chevy's paint job like so many scrambled eggs, while I sucked air and my chest heaved.

Jesse, oh no...

How many hours had I spent with Devin and Jesse, working on the Chevy? Now, in the parking lot, I heard Jesse's laughter inside my head; I recalled his musky scent and thought of the day I'd watched Devin and Jesse make love. It had meant everything to me. Jesse had been so passionate, so full of life. But now...

Oh-h-h, shit.

My face crumpled, and then I sobbed like a five-year-old while classmates filed by Eric and me, shaking their heads. Their faces bore puzzled expressions; they clearly had no idea what had upset me. I'm sure I looked foolish, but I didn't care.

Screw them.

"Come on, Tyler," Eric whispered. "Let's go home."

At Grandma's house, two men in business suits occupied chairs in the living room. One was gray-haired and built like a linebacker; the other was slender, younger. They sipped coffee from cups and saucers. Both rose when I entered the room.

"Tyler," Grandma said, pointing to the older guy, "this is Detective Knox from the sheriff's office."

I put down my books. When I shook hands with Knox, my hand disappeared into his massive paw. Knox jerked a thumb toward the other fellow. "This is my partner, Sergeant Goodall."

I shook hands with Goodall. His eyes were dark and piercing, like he knew my deepest thoughts, and I found it hard to look at him. His face bore a five o'clock shadow and acne scars.

At Knox's request, I sat on the sofa next to my grandma, facing the two cops.

When Knox asked if I'd heard about Jesse's death, I nodded. A vision of Jesse, lying dead in his dad's truck, entered my mind. The back of his skull was blown out and the truck's rear window was splattered with his blood. Immediately, my head ached and my stomach churned. Would I puke again, right in front of everyone?

Knox said, "We're certain this was a suicide; we don't suspect foul play, but..."

I glanced at Grandma; then I returned my gaze to Detective Knox.

"What?" I said.

Knox rearranged his limbs.

"How much do you know about the relationship between Jesse and your half brother?"

I lowered my gaze. Feeling heat in my cheeks, I cleared my throat. Then I looked up.

"They were close friends," I said. "They spent a lot of time together."

Knox looked at my grandmother, then me. After placing his cup and saucer on Grandma's coffee table, he reached into a shirt pocket. Then he produced Jesse's signet ring and gave it to me.

I held the ring in my fingers, staring.

Oh, crap...

"Ever seen it before?" Knox asked.

I nodded.

"Why would Jesse wear a ring with your half brother's initials on it?"

I shrugged and didn't speak. Instead, I handed the ring back.

Knox looked at Goodall, then at the ring. He rubbed the ring between his thumb and index finger.

"Tyler," he said, "how well did you know Jesse?"

I moistened my lips and studied my shoes.

"He was here a lot, working on the car with me and Devin. We talked sometimes. I know he moved here from Jacksonville. He worked in the brickyard with Devin. That's about it."

"Did he or Devin ever mention visiting Jacksonville together?"

I squinted and shook my head.

"You're quite certain?"

"Yeah, why?"

Knox didn't respond. He put the ring back in his shirt pocket; then his knees crackled when he rose. The rest of us stood as well.

Knox looked at Grandma. "Thanks for your time, ma'am. The coffee was a treat."

Grandma walked our visitors to her front screen door,

and I followed them. Grandma and I stood side by side, watching as the two men climbed into an unmarked vehicle, a black Ford sedan with a county plate.

Goodall produced a notebook; he nodded and scribbled while Knox spoke. Knox started the Ford's engine; he shifted gears, and then the Ford's muffler growled as they drove away.

I looked at Grandma.

"What did they want?"

She fingered her pearls, still staring out the screen door.

"Why were they here?" I asked.

Grandma swung her gaze to me.

"From now on, I want you to stay away from Devin."

"How come?"

"He's a bad person, Tyler."

"Why? What's he done?"

"He's a liar and a con artist—a slick one at that."

I crinkled my forehead. What was going on?

Grandma touched my shoulder.

"Promise me you won't associate with Devin, not ever again."

"But—"

"Please, Tyler."

I shoved my hands in my pockets and studied the carpet.

Again, I stood outside my grandma's bedroom door, eavesdropping on her conversation with my mom.

Grandma's voice was strident, angry.

"You and Devin aren't nearly as clever as you might think. Some of those bills in the tobacco tin were printed less than ten years ago. And the information Devin claimed he received from Elmer?"

Grandma hissed.

"You didn't even return my diaries to their proper places on the bookshelf. How stupid do you think I am?"

"Mother, you must understand: I'm trying to improve our circumstances. I am *sick* of the beauty shop, and tired of driving to Daytona in that lousy Dodge. I don't like depending on you for so much, either. Tyler will need money for college, and—"

"That's how you justify deceiving me?"

"Devin would never have received approval from the Council if I—if *we*—hadn't done it."

"And poor Gloria Hagermann," Grandma continued, "she's been deceived as well. That information Devin told her about Helen surely came from Grace Patterson. And that red-haired woman from Ormond Beach, the one who paid me the twenty-five dollars? Go ahead and tell me how *that* was arranged."

My mom didn't say anything.

"Devin's no medium," Grandma said. "He's not clairvoyant. He is simply evil; he uses people, and he'll use you as well. Just wait: your turn will come."

"Mother, Devin's not a bad person, he—"

"Listen to me: that boy, Jesse? He wasn't just Devin's friend; they were *lovers*, Brenda, a pair of sodomites."

My scalp prickled while I flexed my fingers. How did Grandma know?

"Mother, I don't believe it. What makes you think—"

"The boy left a note."

"Who did?"

"Jesse. The police found it with his body."

I shivered in the hallway, feeling like someone had dropped ice cubes down the back of my shirt. Beyond the door, bedsprings creaked. Mom's voice trembled when she spoke.

"What did the note say?"

"I wasn't shown; I only know what Detective Knox told me: Jesse was distraught over Devin's marriage; he didn't want to live without Devin's... attentions."

Tears clouded my eyes. *Poor Jesse...*

Grandma said, "I'd be perfectly justified in asking you to leave this house—I probably should—but I can't punish Tyler for what *you've* done. He's a good boy and certainly deserves better. Have you considered how this will affect him?"

"We'll leave if you'd like," Mom said. "I wouldn't blame you for throwing us out."

Grandma didn't say anything for a long moment. Then she told Mom, "You and Tyler can stay, and I'll try to forgive what you've done. But don't ever mention Devin in my presence, and don't bring him to this house again. Understand?"

Later that evening, I lay in bed, in darkness, staring at the ceiling. My bedroom window stood open. Outside, a breeze stirred fronds of a Sabal palm; the fronds made a sound like cards being shuffled. I felt restless and agitated by the day's events: Jesse's death, Knox's visit, the unmasking of Mom and Devin's not-so-clever ruses.

How much of Devin was a fake and how much was real? Grandma had certainly proved Devin's purported communications with my grandfather a hoax, along with other things, but still...

I recalled how Devin had sensed my presence at the spring, when he'd made love with Jesse. He knew about me tearing the cuff of my blue jeans, about me stealing his underwear and sniffing them. And the breathing exercise he'd taught me had worked, hadn't it?

Now, in my bed, I closed my eyes. I drew a breath and held it ten seconds, then let it out. I repeated the process, over and over, for several minutes. Then, as before, I felt as though my mind had left my body. I floated above

Cassadaga like a bird, looking down at Rev. Patterson's sprawling home with its turret and columned porch, its multiple chimneys.

Detective Knox's Ford stood in Rev. Patterson's driveway.

After descending to ground level, I peeked through a window, into Rev. Patterson's parlor. A brass chandelier with eight arms and shaded lamps lit the room with a golden glow. Devin and Rev. Patterson occupied a leather sofa, Knox a wingback chair, while Sergeant Goodall stood at a marble fireplace, resting his elbow on the mantle. Devin's head was bowed; he held something in his hand. What was it?

I entered the parlor now, passing through the windowpane as if it weren't there, as though my body lacked mass or substance of any kind. Approaching Devin, I stood beside him and bent at the waist. I squinted at the object he held in his fingers. It was Jesse's ring. A tear slid down Devin's cheek; it reflected the chandelier's glow.

I looked at Rev. Patterson. She wore a dressing gown made of quilted material, light blue. Her hands trembled in her lap as she listened to Knox speak, but I couldn't hear what Knox or anyone else in the room said.

Concentrating, I read Rev. Patterson's thoughts. Her mind pictured Devin and Jesse, seated in the Chevrolet, their trousers unzipped, Devin kissing Jesse and touching Jesse between the legs. I sensed a churning in Rev. Patterson's stomach, one similar to the nausea I'd felt in the school parking lot, earlier that day. She rose and scurried to a downstairs bathroom, where she knelt and vomited into the toilet. Another vision entered her head: Rev. Patterson and Devin lay naked in a bed, in an elegantly furnished room. Devin was atop the reverend; he thrust his hips, while she shouted his name at the ceiling.

Now, Rev. Patterson vomited a second time.

Back in the parlor, Knox reached inside his jacket. Then he handed Devin a folded sheet of paper; it appeared to be a photostatic copy. What was it? Devin unfolded the document, he studied its contents before shaking his head. Then he handed the document back to Knox, along with Jesse's ring. Devin said something to Knox. Then Knox looked at Goodall and shrugged. After pocketing the ring and document, Knox rose and hitched his trousers, while Devin remained on the sofa. A crease appeared between Devin's eyebrows; his forearms rested upon his knees, while his hands hung limp.

Knox said something else to Devin. Devin nodded, and then Knox and Goodall strode from the room. They left the house and climbed into the black Ford with the county license tag. Knox took the wheel; he started the engine and flicked on his headlamps. They drove off.

Back in the parlor, Devin remained on the sofa. He stared at the floor, working his jaw from side to side. I tried accessing his thoughts, but couldn't. Was he blocking me intentionally?

If so, why?

Two days after Jesse died, when I came home from school, Devin's Buick sat by the curb. Wearing a sports jacket and dress slacks, Devin sat on the front porch glider; he studied a roadmap. He had crossed a knee with an ankle, and his two-toned shoe twitched.

After sitting beside him, I placed my books on the porch floor. Then I pointed to the map.

"Taking a trip?"

He nodded; then he folded the map and set it aside.

"Where?" I said.

He shrugged. "I haven't decided, but I'm leaving Cassadaga for good; that much is certain."

My eyes clouded. Devin would leave? He wouldn't come back?

I said, "What about Rev. Patterson?"

He drew a breath; then he let it out, while his shoulders sagged. "She's having our marriage annulled, Ty."

"Because of Jesse?"

"Partly. And because the cops think I killed that girl, the one they found at the sawmill. Jesse said so in his suicide note."

I studied my shoes and licked my lips. I looked at Devin and asked him, "Did you and Jesse ever visit Jacksonville?"

Devin asked why I wanted to know.

"Detective Knox asked me about it."

Devin looked at my Chevy in the driveway. Then he returned his gaze to me. "We went many places in that car, Tyler."

"Are you running from the law? Is that why you're leaving?"

Devin shook his head. "They have nothing to prove I murdered that child. Jesse's note can't be used in court; it's hearsay, but just the same, I can't stay here. I'll have no place to live and no job prospects."

For a moment, I thought of asking Devin to take me with him. Things had changed so much since he'd come to Cassadaga; I owed most everything good in my life to Devin. But leaving wouldn't make sense, would it? I had my mom and grandma to think about. There was my education to consider. And, of course, there was Eric.

Devin rose. "I'd better go," he said, "before Grandma comes home. I only wanted to say goodbye before I left."

I nodded. My eyes watered when I rose. I flung my arms around Devin's neck, and then Devin hugged me while I wept.

"Sh-h-h-h," he whispered. "Things will be okay; you'll see."

Minutes later, I wiped snot from my upper lip, while I watched him drive away. There were so many things I'd wanted to know, so many questions I'd wanted to ask Devin, but didn't. Had he truly loved Jesse? Had he only married Rev. Patterson for her money? Did he really possess spiritual powers, or was that all bunk? And *had* he killed that girl? If so, why? Just to appear on television?

I closed my eyes and thought of the day I'd first taken Devin to the spring, when I'd seen him naked and longed to touch him. Now, it would never happen, would it? For the rest of my life, I'd wonder how it would have felt to share intimacy with Devin.

Stop, Tyler.

You have to let go...

After opening my eyes, I squared my shoulders. I turned on my heel, bent at the waist, and lifted my books from Grandma's porch floor.

Then I entered her house.

CHAPTER SIXTEEN

In mid-October, I stood in a hallway just outside our school's gymnasium. I fixed my gaze on a sign-up sheet tacked to a bulletin board. If I wanted to try out for Deland High's basketball team, I'd need to write my name on the sheet.

I rubbed my index finger against my thumb. Was I really good enough to make the cut? Sure, I'd practiced religiously, every day: my ball handling, my free throws, and my jump shot. But I'd never played in a real game with four teammates and five opponents. If I tried, would I make a fool out of myself in front of everyone?

Two guys brushed past me, both half a head taller than me. Their voices were deep-pitched, and one guy had a five o'clock shadow. They traded insults while scribbling their names on the sign-up sheet. I studied their big hands and feet, and the muscles in their forearms.

I'd look like a stick figure, a total shrimp, standing next to them at tryouts. Who am I kidding?

I hung my head and walked away.

Christmastime came, and school let out for two weeks. One cold front after another rolled across northeast

Florida; temperatures sometimes dropped below freezing during the night and often did not rise above fifty degrees during the day. The wind blew steadily, and the sky remained overcast. Many evenings, I'd start a blaze in our living room fireplace, using cordwood Grandma kept under a canvas tarp behind the garage. I'd tote wood into the house, then use newspaper and sap-laden splinters as kindling. I'd get a nice fire going. Then I'd sit before the hearth, reading a book with a blanket wrapped about my shoulders.

By now, the Florida maples in my grandma's yard had lost their rust-colored leaves. One afternoon, I raked them into a pile and burned them, using kerosene as lighter fluid. I didn't mind. I couldn't swim at the spring; the weather was too nasty. Eric's family had left town for the holidays, and I had no one to spend time with. Raking leaves gave me something to do; it gave me time to think about the past and where my life was headed.

I thought of Devin. I wondered what he was up to, and where he lived now. My mom had severed all communications with Devin, right after the scandal of Jesse's suicide came to light. Now that her conspiracy with Devin had failed, I guess he no longer served a useful purpose in Mom's life. She'd lost interest in him, I suppose.

It bewildered me, how little love existed between the two of them, and sometimes I wondered just how much my mother loved *me*. Was I nothing more than an obligation she was forced to discharge, like paying taxes or doing laundry?

Another thing: did Devin care for me? I wanted to believe he did, but he hadn't even sent me a postcard since his departure.

By now, of course, I knew Devin wasn't as perfect as I'd once thought, but I still loved him, despite his deceptions. He was, after all, my half brother. And I still thought he was the most beautiful man I'd ever laid eyes on. I frequently lay in bed at night, thinking of Devin's hair and eyes, his smooth skin and rippling muscles. A few times I tried contacting him telepathically, using the breathing technique he'd taught me, but I had no success. Was Devin deliberately ignoring my attempts? Had he forgotten me entirely? Would I never see him again?

While raking and burning, I spent a good deal of time pondering my relationship with Eric too. Was it everything it should be? He'd told me dozens of times how much he loved me. And I'd said the same thing to him. But exactly what did the "love" between us mean?

I'd read plenty of novels where characters fell in love: Hemingway's *For Whom the Bell Tolls*, Ayn Rand's *Atlas Shrugged*, Margaret Mitchell's *Gone with the Wind*. I even procured a copy of Gore Vidal's novel, *The City and the Pillar*, a story of homosexual love between two men. It was banned from our school, so I had to steal the book from Stetson University's library in Deland.

In *For Whom the Bell Tolls*, after making love with his girlfriend, Pilar, Robert Jordan asks her, "But did thee feel the earth move?"

Pilar says yes, it did.

Well.

Sex with Eric was very good—I always looked forward to it—but I couldn't say *I* ever felt the earth move, either during or after our lovemaking sessions. Where was the pulse-quickening, all-consuming desire experienced by characters in these books? My relationship with Eric was comfortable, sure, but I felt no fire inside me, no desperate need for Eric's presence. Was this my fault? Was it Eric's? Maybe the authors of these books had simply exaggerated the intensity of romantic love, in order to sell more books.

Or, maybe true romantic love wasn't possible between two males. Maybe we queers only got half a loaf. In *The City and the Pillar*, Sullivan tells his lover, Jim, ". . . you're never going to fit into this sort of relationship, and so the sooner you find your way to something else, the better it'll be for you."

Did I "fit into" my relationship with Eric? Or did I need to "find my way to something else"?

If so, what?

Christmas morning, I woke shortly after sunrise. Golden light slanted into my room through my eastern window, falling upon a creased and coffee-stained envelope; it rested on my nightstand. My name appeared on the envelope in red ink, in squiggly cursive handwriting.

inkling my forehead, I brought my feet to the floor; I rubbed sleep from my eyes with my knuckles. Then I opened the envelope. Inside was a gift certificate for fifty dollars from a Daytona Beach sporting goods store and a note scribbled on a sheet of foolscap:

Ty:
Buy yourself a new pair of basketball sneakers.
Love, Devin

Glancing about the room, I noticed a double-hung window was slightly cracked open. I walked to the window, raised it, and peered left and right. I studied a sectioned drainage pipe; it descended from a rain gutter on the roof, all the way to the ground, passing by the window. More than one joint on the pipe was caked with orange clay from Grandma's yard.

I pictured Devin scaling the pipe, playing Santa Claus in the darkness, moving silent as a cat, and creeping across my bedroom floor.

A grin crossed my face.

He hasn't forgotten me, after all, has he?

CHAPTER SEVENTEEN

O n a warm afternoon in late May, toward the end of my sophomore year, Eric Rupp sat beside me in the Chevy's front seat. Sunlight hammered the Chevy's hood. We had parked behind the warehouse, just off the County Road, and then we made love.

Now, while we buttoned our shirts, Eric said, "I have bad news."

I looked at him, and he looked at me.

I crinkled my forehead. "What?"

Eric moistened his lips. He drew a breath and gave his attention to the windshield.

"My folks sold their business. We're moving to Virginia, to a town called Alexandria, as soon as the school year ends. My mom's parents live there."

I felt as if Eric had punched me in the stomach. I opened my mouth to say something, but nothing came out. My eyes clouded with tears. For over a year, he'd been my lover and confidant. Okay, our relationship had been far from perfect, but I still felt closer to Eric than to anyone else in the world.

Now he would *leave*?

"I'm sorry, Ty. If it were up to me..."

I thrust my face into my hands and wept. My body shook like a palm frond in a thunderstorm. I felt as though someone had sliced me open, and now they were tearing my guts from my body, one handful at a time. My voice quivered when I spoke.

"It's not fair. You *can't* leave me like this. I thought we'd spend our lives together. Who will I visit the spring with? Who will I camp with? And where will I ever find another person like you?"

Eric put his arm around my shoulders.

"Sh-h-h-h," he whispered. "It'll work out."

Two weeks later, we said our goodbyes at the spring, after making love on my blanket. Then I drove Eric home. I watched him climb the steps to his screened front porch. He turned to me and waved, one last time, and then he was gone. Just like that.

Eric's departure left me lonely and morose. School was out for summer break, and for several days, I never left Grandma's house. I didn't even visit the spring because I knew going there would only worsen the hurt from my loss of Eric. I read magazines, wrote in my journal, and worked a jigsaw puzzle or two. Zits erupted on my forehead. I kept forgetting to scrub my teeth or brush my hair, or even bathe.

"You look like a hobo," my Mom told me one day. "Is there something wrong?"

But I couldn't very well tell her I was pining for Eric, now could I?

One afternoon in mid-June, my grandmother returned from her day's work. I lay upon the living room sofa in my stocking feet, staring at the ceiling and thinking of Eric. A half-eaten sandwich rested on the coffee table, next to an empty Coca-Cola bottle. On a windowsill, a box fan hummed; it fluttered the pages of a *Life* magazine I'd read earlier.

My grandmother put down her purse on the little table by our front door. Then she placed her hands on her hips.

"Are you planning on spending all summer doing nothing?" she asked.

I shrugged and didn't say anything.

Grandma continued.

"I passed the Sinclair station on my way home today, the one on Marion Street. A sign in the window says they're looking for an attendant to pump gas. Why don't you pay them a visit?"

I made a face.

"I don't know much about cars," I said. "Why would they hire me?"

Grandma looked at me like I was a needle she planned to thread.

"There's only one way to find out, now isn't there?"

I landed the Sinclair job after a brief interview with the station's owner, Cletis Hyde. It seemed his biggest concern was whether or not I could make correct change when patrons paid cash for gas and other merchandise.

"Show up on time," Cletis told me. "Be respectful toward our customers, and don't steal from the cash register. Keep yourself busy, and we'll get along fine, you and me."

I pumped gas and cleaned windshields. I fixed flat tires and performed oil changes. Cletis was a skinny, balding guy with horn-rimmed eyeglasses and tufts of hair growing out of his ears. He nicknamed me "Slick." When he wasn't whistling, he sang naughty limericks. ("There was a young lady named Alice, who used dynamite as a phallus...") Cletis was a chain smoker; the tips of his fingers bore tobacco stains, and his teeth were crooked and yellow.

Cletis' wife Bessie, a hefty woman with thinning hair and a mole on her cheek the size of an M&M, kept the station's books. She wrote checks, made bank deposits, and filed the station's sales tax reports with the Florida Department of Revenue. My first day on the job, she'd made it clear I wasn't to touch the financial materials she kept in drawers of a metal desk in the station's cramped office.

Cletis knew his way around cars; he could fix most any problem.

The other mechanic, Blon O'Keefe, was plenty good with cars himself; he could tune an engine in less than thirty minutes. Blon was foul-mouthed; he'd once been Rev. Patterson's paramour, and he made no secret of it.

One day, he told me, "I kid you not, Ty: that bitch can hump."

Blon was in his late twenties. Broad-shouldered and athletic, he had ice-blue eyes and a shock of yellow hair. He was twenty-eight, and still unmarried. At six-four, he towered over me. He had played varsity football, baseball, and basketball for Deland High School, as a teenager, and he was quick. He kept a backboard and goal nailed to a power pole on the Sinclair property. When business was slow, we'd often play one-on-one, using a leather ball Blon kept at the station. Cletis would sit in the shade of the station's lube bay, smoking unfiltered Camels and watching us sweat.

Blon taught me how to execute a reverse layup, something I'd never seen before.

"Get yourself underneath the goal—to one side or the other—and facing away from the backboard. When you see an opening, pivot and take a step, then *lift* the ball into the air; give it some spin and bank it into the goal. You'll be surprised how many points you can score."

I practiced the maneuver for hours at home, and in

time, I mastered the reverse layup, adding it to my quiver of moves.

Work at the Sinclair station could be brutal at times, especially during afternoons. By midday, the temperature often reached ninety-five, and the humidity was nearly as high. My pea-green coveralls, with their purple Dinosaur patch, would stick to my sternum. The coveralls would cling to the small of my back while I raised hoods, to check oil levels and fill battery cells with distilled water. The gas pumps weren't shaded, so I'd use a rag to protect my hand when I lifted nozzles and unscrewed gas caps. The station's concrete apron was hot as an anvil; I could feel its heat through the soles of my work boots. Surfaces of cars I serviced would scorch my skin whenever I'd inadvertently brush up against them.

Afternoon rainstorms were blessings. They mostly came from the north, portended by a cool breeze, and I could smell the rain well before it arrived. Thunder would rumble in the distance, and lightning would skitter across the darkening sky. Charcoal-colored clouds would billow above us. Then the rain would come, pounding the station's roof and sheeting off the eaves. It would rat-a-tat on the apron and pumps, before streaming toward the County Road's drainage ditches. In the bays, Cletis and Blon would flick on their utility lights and hang them from hoods of the cars they worked on. I would stand alongside them, watching and asking questions, learning something new every time: how to patch a leaky radiator with solder, how to locate an electrical short, how to replace wheel bearings and so forth.

I worked five days a week. Sundays we were closed, and I took Tuesdays off. Cletis paid every Friday, and it was nice having spending money. Often, on Saturday nights, I'd drive to Daytona Beach, where I'd walk the main drag, past the bars and T-shirt shops, the tattoo parlors and pool halls. I'd admire attractive guys in their chinos and Madras shirts, and I'd wonder if I would ever have another boyfriend.

The day we'd last visited the spring, Eric promised he'd write me once a week.

"You do the same," he said. "It's important we stay in touch, 'cause one day I'll be back."

But after we'd exchanged a few letters, Eric stopped writing altogether. I wasn't surprised; he'd never been a "correspondence" kind of guy, and I soon realized I wouldn't hear from him again. What we'd shared was now finished, and this fact saddened me to no end.

Sometimes I longed for Eric's touch so badly my stomach ached. I'd stand in the Sinclair's lube bay, emptying a car's oil pan, and I'd daydream about lovemaking with Eric. I'd recall the times we had parked the Chevy on the way home from school, and then held each other. I would close my eyes and travel back in time. I'd feel Eric's lips pressed to mine, his hand on the back of my neck. But then a car would approach the pumps out front. The driver would beep his horn, and I'd flutter my eyelids. My reverie would float away like a butterfly.

Let go, Tyler.

You have to let go...

The Sinclair station didn't just sell gasoline and batteries. A cigarette machine offered Winstons, Camels, Salems, Chesterfields, and several other brands. We sold candy bars, mints, chewing gum, peanut butter crackers, cough drops, and Life Savers, all displayed in a glass case inside the office.

The smokes and other goodies were supplied to us on a weekly basis by Volusia Cigar Company, a wholesaler in Daytona Beach. Every so often, a man named Byron Teague, owner of Volusia Cigar, would visit the station to collect a check from Bessie, and to discuss any new products Cletis might want to sell our customers.

Teague was a taciturn, slender man my height, with a cleft chin and a perpetual five o'clock shadow. He always wore the same outfit: an open-neck, short-sleeved white shirt, black slacks, scuffed brogues, and a black straw fedora with a striped band. His horn-rimmed eyeglasses—also black—had thick lenses; they gave his eyes a bugged-out appearance. When he wasn't smoking Chesterfields, he chewed gum.

I never once saw him smile or laugh.

Teague's voice was a scratchy tenor, his drawl thick, and he always addressed me as "boy" when he came to the station. He drove a gleaming Cadillac Fleetwood, nearly the length of a freight car, with stacked headlights and a huge chrome grille that made me squint when he'd pull onto the Sinclair's apron.

"Fill 'er up, boy," he'd say to me, "and gimme the works."

I'd top off his tank, check his oil, clean his windshield, and check the pressure in his white sidewall tires. He'd always inspect the windshield before he left, looking for streaks or bugs I'd missed. If he wasn't satisfied, he'd make me clean the glass a second time, puffing away on his cigarette or smacking his gum while I squirted and wiped, squirted and wiped.

One afternoon, after Teague left the station, I joined Cletis in the lube bay, where he installed a new master cylinder in a Nash Rambler. I felt irritated, as Teague had insisted I fill his windshield washer reservoir, and then clean his *rear* window, in addition to my normal services. The day was blistering hot; I sweated from my labors. My coveralls stuck to my chest and the small of my back.

Cletis used a socket wrench to tighten bolts, and the ratcheting sound only worsened my mood.

"Do you like Mr. Teague?" I asked Cletis.

After halting his work, Cletis looked up at me like I was crazy.

"Nobody likes Byron Teague."

"Then how come you do business with him?"

Cletis wiped grease from his hands, using a rag. His face made an expression like he'd just sucked juice from a lemon.

"Teague's an influential man in these parts, both in business and politics; he's not someone you want as an enemy. Let's just say it makes sense to stay on his good side."

I crinkled my forehead. "I don't understand."

Cletis looked left and right; then his gaze met mine. He spoke in a near-whisper.

"Teague's high up in the Ku Klux. If a Volusia County man wants to run for public office—county judge, legislature, tax collector, or whatever—he needs Teague's blessing."

Cletis returned his rag to his back pocket.

"Now, I could earn a better profit if I bought merchandise from another wholesaler, but then my truck tires would be ice-picked or my dog might be poisoned. Understand?"

I nodded, thinking of the Confederate flag license plate Teague displayed on his Fleetwood's front bumper.

Cletis said, "All this talk of sending colored kids to school with whites? It won't happen in Volusia County, I guarantee it; not as long as Byron Teague draws breath. He's a mean man, Tyler. You're best off saying as little as possible when he's around."

Rubbing my chin with a knuckle, I tried to imagine Teague in one of those silly Klan outfits I'd seen in television documentaries: the pointed hoods and the gowns with floppy sleeves. I hadn't even realized the Ku Klux Klan existed in Volusia County.

Was the Klan something I should even care about?

CHAPTER EIGHTEEN

While working at the station, I made acquaintance with Peter Bohannon, band teacher at the junior high school I'd attended in Orange City. Since I had never played an instrument, I hadn't known Mr. Bohannon while attending his school. But now he was a regular customer at the Sinclair station. He always talked to me while I filled his gas tank, while I put air in his tires, and washed his windshield.

After we spoke a few times, he said, "Ty, I think you're old enough to call me Peter."

Thereafter, I did.

A graduate of Florida State University, Peter was only a few years out of college. He was tall and slender, and he kept his hair in place with Brylcreem. His green eyes had a way of boring into me when our gazes met. The way he looked at me made me so nervous I'd always glance away, after a few seconds. Peter wore long-sleeved, Oxford cloth shirts, khaki pants, and penny loafers shiny as mirrors. Or sometimes he wore a Banlon shirt and jeans with the cuffs rolled up a couple of inches. When he smiled, his lips would fold back, revealing two rows of perfect teeth, white as porcelain. His voice was deep like Devin's, easy on the ears, and he was a good listener too. He seemed interested in my views on issues of the day.

I found it easy to talk with Peter on any number of subjects. Aside from my teachers at school, I knew no one with a college degree, and I'd often ask Peter questions about university life. What was it like, moving away from home and living in a dormitory? How many hours did a guy have to study each day, to keep up? And how should I decide on a major?

Peter probably came by the station twice a week, usually around 4:00 p.m., just after summer band practice had ended. He'd lean against the fender of his Ford Galaxy while I topped off his tank, and we'd chat.

One Friday afternoon, Peter asked what I would do with my weekend.

I shrugged. "Nothing much."

Peter said, "I'll see a film in Daytona tomorrow night—*The Sand Pebbles* with Steve McQueen. Care to join me?"

The invitation took me by surprise. Peter was an adult, an educator respected in our community. Me? I was just a high school kid, a gas pump jockey. I felt flattered an adult with a college education actually wanted my company.

I said, "Sure." After I jotted my address on the back of an envelope, we agreed Peter would pick me up at quarter 'til seven, the following day.

Saturday evening, I showered and shampooed. I scrubbed my nails with an old toothbrush, to get at the grease beneath them. I styled my hair with tonic, and wore my best outfit: a Madras shirt over an undershirt, chinos, white socks, and penny loafers. When I descended the stairs, counting the money in my wallet, my mom sat in an easy chair; soaking her feet in her Epsom salts solution. She wolf-whistled when she saw me.

"Big date tonight?"

I chuckled and shook my head. Then I explained what was up.

Mom crinkled her forehead. "How old is this man?"

"Twenty-four."

She puckered one side of her face. "Doesn't he have any friends his own age?"

I shrugged and didn't answer her question. Moments later, Peter pulled to the curb out front, his car engine purring. The sun was already behind the western tree line, and Peter had switched on his parking lights. His radio played a jazz tune, something by Chet Baker.

Mom peered out a window; she studied Peter's car. "What time should I expect you?" she asked.

I shrugged. "It's a long film—three hours. Don't wait up."

After bounding down the front porch steps, I thrust my head through the Galaxy's open passenger window. I greeted Peter with a grin.

He raised a palm and smiled his porcelain smile. "Evening, Ty; hop in."

I felt quite the adult, cruising down the highway toward Daytona with Peter. We talked about his day at school, about *The Sand Pebbles*, and how the film was Oscar-nominated for Best Picture. We talked about my work, as well.

"The heat's bothersome," I told Peter, "but I've learned a lot from Cletis and Blon. They don't treat me like I'm a kid, and I appreciate it."

"You're how old?" Peter said.

"I'll be seventeen in a few weeks."

Peter nodded, looking at me. "Then you're certainly not a 'kid,' Tyler."

Heat rose in my cheeks and I looked away. I felt flattered Peter considered me his equal, and not some punk who only tagged along.

How cool is this?

In Daytona, we dined at a fast food place, munching

on burgers and fries, and sipping from soda cups. Peter explained how he'd been raised in Ft. Lauderdale, where his folks owned a marina.

"I grew up around boats. I sure miss living near the ocean."

I nodded.

"One day I'll leave Cassadaga," I said. "Maybe I'll live in St. Augustine or New Smyrna—someplace I can walk the beach every day, if I want to."

The Seaside Movie Theater was Daytona's finest venue at the time, with a columned entrance looking much like a Greek temple. Just off US Highway 1, it stood less than a block from the Intracoastal Waterway. I smelled the Waterway's briny scent, when we parked the Galaxy and strode down the sidewalk. We passed under streetlamps; their glow reflected in our penny loafers.

At the ticket booth, Peter insisted on paying for both of us.

"This was my idea," he said, "so it's my treat."

The Sand Pebbles was pretty good. Set in 1926 China, it focused on the troubled crew of a US Navy gunboat. Besides McQueen, I knew many of the film's cast: Richard Crenna, Candice Bergen, Richard Attenborough, and Ford Rainey. During intermission, Peter and I visited the men's room; we peed side by side at urinals. Then Peter bought us Cokes and popcorn.

Already, I felt at ease in Peter's company. While we waited for the movie to resume, Peter asked me questions. He thought McQueen was one of America's great actors. Did I agree? What did I think about the issues of racism addressed in the movie? In the faculty lounge at Peter's workplace, there was talk Volusia County schools would soon be integrated, by order of the federal court in Jacksonville. How would I feel about going to school with Negroes?

I took my time answering; I didn't want to say something foolish or immature. Peter listened as I spoke, rubbing his chin and nodding from time to time.

Then, about an hour into the film's second half, something unexpected happened: Peter shifted position, and the springs in his seat creaked. He reached across the armrest between us. Then he placed his hand on my thigh, a little above my knee.

My pulse accelerated. I glanced at Peter from the corner of my eye. His gaze was fixed on the movie screen; when he moistened his lips, they glistened. I shifted my gaze to his hand; I could barely see it in the darkened auditorium. Had anyone noticed what Peter was up to? And how should I react?

I liked Peter and found him attractive enough, but the pass he was making caught me totally off guard. I'd never even suspected he was gay, but he seemed to know *I* was, and I wasn't sure how I felt about that. Was my queerness so obvious?

I kept still in my seat. My only movement was the rise and fall of my chest when I breathed. Minutes passed; then Peter's hand inched its way up my leg, toward my crotch.

Surely he won't touch me there? Not in the middle of a theater?

I worked my jaw and flexed my toes while Peter's hand crept toward my zipper.

Do something, Tyler.

Seizing Peter's wrist, I turned my head and looked at him. He looked at me and winked. Then he gave me a cute little smile, like we were conspirators in a devious plot no one else knew of.

My stomach churned. Suddenly, I felt ambushed. I felt exploited and oh so silly. For a second, I felt like crying. I'd been played for a fool, hadn't I? Peter didn't consider me an adult or an equal; that's not why he'd invited me to join him, was it?

He only wanted to get in my pants

My gaze still fixed on Peter's, I shook my head as subtly as I could. Then I lifted his hand from my thigh and placed it on the armrest.

Peter frowned. After returning his gaze to the screen, he gave his attention to *The Sand Pebbles*, and he did not touch me again. I was so shook up I found it hard to concentrate on the movie. In truth, I couldn't wait for it to end.

We said little to each other during our ride back to Cassadaga. Peter switched on the radio, and we both kept our gazes on the windshield.

When he pulled to the curb in front of Grandma's, I told him, "Thanks for the movie. I enjoyed it."

Peter looked into his lap and nodded, but he didn't say anything when I left the car.

I never saw Peter again.

CHAPTER NINETEEN

The fall of my junior year, I gathered my courage and signed up to try out for Deland High School's basketball team. I was six feet tall now. I'd added to muscle to my frame over summer, so I figured I could hold my own against guys my size or bigger.

The coach was Raymond Ebersole, a former US Marine who'd once played basketball for Georgia Tech. Ebersole was a middle-aged, gum-chewing, barrel-chested man with big shoulders, a flat belly, and hands like paws. His gravelly drawl made me wince whenever he barked at someone. Deep creases in his cheeks and forehead made his face resemble a well-used catcher's mitt. His gray eyes lent his visage a spooky quality. Ebersole always wore a white T-shirt damp in the armpits, black football shorts that showed off his powerful legs, and canvas, high-top sneakers. A whistle hung from his neck on a braided cord.

Tryouts occurred in the school's gymnasium, on a humid Tuesday afternoon. The place stank of sweat, liniment, canvas sneakers, and leather. Two dozen boys sat in the bleachers, me among them, all of us wearing numbered pieces of paper safety-pinned to the backs of our shirts. At one end of the court, six seniors—returners from last year's squad—practiced their jump shots.

Ebersole stood before the bleachers, clipboard in

hand, calling out names from the tryout sheet, noting the number on each guy's back. When he called my name, I raised my hand and told him I was number fourteen. Ebersole looked at me like I was something he might buy at a garage sale. His icy stare scared me. Despite the gym's heat, Ebersole's gaze made me shiver, and I quickly looked away. Thereafter, each time his gaze swung to mine, I'd lower my chin and study my shoes.

After he'd finished roll call, Ebersole tossed the clipboard to the team's manager, Mike Monroe, a skinny kid with pimples and horn-rimmed eyeglasses. Monroe wore dress slacks and a short-sleeve white shirt. He kept a pen caddy in his shirt pocket. A slide rule hung from his belt in a leather scabbard.

Ebersole crossed his arms at his chest. While scanning faces in the bleachers, he said, "Athletic association rules allow me twelve players only." Then he jerked a thumb toward the seniors on the court. "Those guys have already made the team; that leaves six slots to fill, so don't get your hopes up. Most of you will not—I repeat, will *not*—make the cut.

"What am I looking for? Speed, for one thing. Good ball handling's another. I want men who can drive to the basket and lay it up, consistently. I want smooth jump shots, good free-throw percentages, and *defense*. I want *tenacious*, dogged defense."

He pointed toward his seniors again. "Just ask those pudwhackers. They'll tell you something: I won't tolerate laziness. I want a hundred percent from every player, every time he steps onto the court. No exceptions, no excuses."

Ebersole pointed at a lanky kid in the bleachers, a boy taller than me with straw-colored hair falling into his eyes.

"What's your name again?"

"Hobgood, sir."

"During the past week, how many hours did you practice each day?"

Hobgood looked about him, as if seeking an acceptable response from the guys around him. Then Hobgood looked at Ebersole and shrugged.

"One or two, I guess."

Ebersole squinted; he puckered one side of his beefy face, while he shook his head.

"One or two, you *guess*?"

Hobgood licked his lips and didn't say anything. He studied his sneakers instead.

Ebersole paced the floor, jabbing the air with his index finger. "In my book, three hours of practice per day is the minimum required. Three hours are what is necessary if you want to hone your skills, and if you want to help our team win games. If you can't make that sort of commitment, well..." Ebersole pointed to the gym's double doors; a red Exit sign glowed above them. "Leave now."

On the court, Ebersole had us form two lines on either side of the key, each with an equal number of boys. A guy in the left line would dribble toward the goal; he'd attempt a layup. Then he'd go to the rear of the other line. A guy at the head of the right line would do the same, joining the left line after his layup. Half the guys missed their first two attempts. Many seemed more nervous than I, chewing hangnails as they waited their turns. I kept my mind focused on the backboard and my dribbling.

I ignored everyone around me; I pretended I played on Grandma's driveway, and I made both my initial layups. The ball ricocheted off the backboard; each time it swished through the net.

Ebersole stood at the court's edge, chewing his gum. He watched and made comments to Monroe, who nodded and scribbled notes on the clipboard.

While I dribbled toward the backboard for my third attempt, Ebersole hollered at me.

"Pick up the pace. This is basketball, not croquet."

His comment distracted me, and I flubbed the shot. My cheeks flamed while I rejoined a layup line.

You're an idiot, Tyler, a bumbling fool. But I calmed down and made my fourth attempt, leaping a bit higher than before and *lifting* the ball toward the backboard, like it was a newborn infant—a term Blon had always used when teaching me.

I swung a fist when the ball hissed through the goal.

That's better.

Ebersole blew his whistle when the last boy made his fourth attempt.

"Enough with the layups. Now we'll play a little two-on-two with the big boys."

Ebersole pointed at two seniors. "Hartmann, Scheevers, guard the goal." Then Ebersole told the remaining seniors, "You crotch-scratchers grab a seat."

We formed two lines. The guys at the head of both lines entered the half court with a ball, dribbling, passing it back and forth, and approaching the defenders. One kid was chunky, his legs thick, his movements plodding. The other kid was skinny as a fence post, with a mop of dark, curly hair. Hartmann, one of the seniors, was easily six-four, with huge hands and feet. Mike Scheevers was shorter, but quick. He moved away from the goal, approaching the chunky boy who dribbled. Scheevers kept lunging at the kid, swiping at the ball, and the kid quickly grew flustered; he tried dribbling past Scheevers but couldn't, so he passed it to his partner.

"We don't have all day," Ebersole hollered. "Work it toward the goal."

The skinny kid charged the goal—his ball handling

was pretty good—but when he tried a jump shot, about twelve feet from the goal, Hartmann stuffed him, slapping the ball so hard it bounced into the bleachers.

And so it went.

I was paired with a guy I didn't know. A bit taller than me, with broad shoulders and a lanky frame, his auburn hair was straight as straw and it fell into his eyes. We entered the half court with my partner dribbling. Scheevers approached him, arms raised, his gaze fixed on the ball, but just as Scheevers lunged for the ball, the kid shifted direction and blew past Scheevers. Scheevers tripped over his own feet and fell to the hardwood. The kid signaled me to move toward the left side of the goal, while he approached Hartmann, who faced him with his hands raised, ready to block my partner's shot.

The kid faked left, then moved to his right, dribbling furiously. He bent his knees and raised the ball, preparing to jump shoot, it appeared. But when he sprang into the air, he flicked the ball to me instead. Unguarded, I took two steps toward the goal and laid up the ball, an easy two pointer.

The guys in the tryout lines cheered, while the seniors in the bleachers shouted insults at Scheevers.

Over the next two hours, the process repeated itself, over and over. Ebersole rotated his six seniors on the court. I remained paired with the auburn-haired kid, and we quickly found ourselves a rhythm, working the ball in carefully, passing it back and forth, drawing out one defender, then blowing past him and challenging the other senior defending the goal. My partner wasn't as quick as me, but his jump shot was lethal and his rebounding was aggressive. He didn't seem the least bit intimidated by seniors larger than him. Of course, we didn't score every time we got the ball, but we won more matchups than we lost.

On our final possession, with all four of us crowding the goal, I executed a reverse layup. It bounced off the backboard and bobbled about inside the goal's rim before dropping through the net—not a perfect maneuver, but it worked.

I felt bad for some of the kids trying out. Many were not good ball handlers, others were simply too slow. But a few were indisputably varsity material, and everyone, I think, sensed this. A guy named Mark Maggert, a pass receiver on our school's football team, looked as comfortable on the court as he would have been in his living room. He ran circles around the seniors, made every layup he attempted. And he wasn't a ball hog. He'd set up shots for his partner to make, even when he had a clear shot himself.

Clever. He's showing Ebersole he's a team player.

Another guy I knew from English class, Charles Sweeney, could jump like nobody's business. He'd spring into the air and arc the ball toward the goal, his wrist flopping forward, index finger pointing at his target. Though I guessed he was five-ten at most, he often out-rebounded guys taller than him, including Hartmann. Sweeney dribbled like the ball was part of his body; he never even looked at it while maneuvering about the court, moving left, then right. His intentions were completely unpredictable.

After an hour, the seniors switched to offense, and the guys trying out played defense.

"Get those arms up," Ebersole hollered at two kids trying to guard much larger seniors. "Hustle, hustle, hustle, goddamnit."

Afterward, while the seniors went to the locker room, the rest of us sat in the bleachers, our T-shirts sticking to our backs, sweat beading on our upper lips, while Ebersole and Mike Monroe stood before us. Ebersole scratched his chest and looked us over like we were steaks in a butcher shop's display case.

"I know what you're all wondering," he said. "When will Coach decide who makes the cut and who doesn't?" Ebersole looked down at his sneakers; he kicked hardwood with a toe. Then he raised his chin.

"I'm a man who makes his decisions carefully, but quickly. I don't pussyfoot around. I can tell you right now, some of you guys had no business coming here; you're too green and you haven't practiced nearly enough. But I suppose there are six of you who stand *some* chance of learning the art of this game."

Ebersole pointed to the gymnasium doors. "Thursday after school, I'll post the team roster on the bulletin board, right out there. I'm warning you: if you're name *is* on the list, you may live to regret it. You'll work harder for me than you've ever worked in your life. Every waking hour of your day, when you're not doing schoolwork, you'll think about basketball. At night you'll *dream* about basketball. Any slacking, any loss of concentration, and I'll yank you from the team; it's a promise."

Ebersole pointed a finger, right at me. His gaze bore into mine.

"If you're not prepared to give me one hundred percent, now's your chance to leave."

I lowered my chin and stared at the sweat-soaked number on the back of a boy seated in front of me. I felt entirely unnerved by Ebersole's attentions. All I could think was, *Am I good enough?*

Afterward, in the school parking lot, a scratchy voice cried to me.

"Hey, wait up." The voice belonged to the auburn-haired kid, my two-on-two partner. He also carried a gym bag. He approached with a lazy stride, while brushing his bangs from his face. When he drew near, I noticed his hazel eyes. Freckles peppered his cheeks and his oversized nose as well; the freckles looked like confetti.

He said, "How do you think we did?"

I shrugged. "Better than most, I think."

After shifting his bag to his left hand, he extended his right. "I'm Jacob Rachinoff."

Rachinoff? What kind of a name is that?

We shook. His hand felt warm and moist, and his grip was firm.

I told him my name. Then I said, "I've never seen you at school before."

He nodded. "That's 'cause we've just moved here from Skokie. My dad bought a pharmacy business, here in Deland."

I said I'd never heard of Skokie. "Where is it?"

"Up north, near Chicago."

When Jacob said "Chicago," he pronounced it "Shi-*caw*-gah."

"That your car?" he asked, pointing at the Chevy.

I nodded; I told Jacob it was a gift from my older brother.

"Lucky you," he said while his gaze drifted over the Chevy's shiny surfaces. "I'm on foot."

I jerked a thumb. "Hop in, and I'll give you a ride"

On the way to Jacob's house, we stopped at a fast food place to purchase sodas and fries. Then we sat at an outdoor, concrete table, yakking away. Beyond the curb, early evening traffic roared past. We talked about the tryout session, about Ebersole, and our classes at school. Jacob was an animated guy; his big hands were always on the move, pointing here and there, slapping the tabletop, or twirling at the wrists. He talked about Skokie and how its population was largely Jewish.

"I attended Fasman Yeshiva High," he said. "It's for boys only, strictly Orthodox."

I told Jacob I'd never met a Jew before, not that I knew of.

"I'm not surprised. The closest temple's in Orlando—an hour's drive for my family every Saturday. I think we might be the only Jews in Volusia County."

I told Jacob I liked his style on the court. "Where'd you learn?"

"From a neighbor in Skokie, Si Grossmann, the first Jew ever to play for Illinois State. He kept a backboard on a post at the edge of his driveway. One day, I watched him practice and he tossed me the ball. He said, 'Jacob, you're a tall boy, with long arms and big hands; you're built for this sport.' He'd practice with me most every afternoon. Then, on Sundays, he'd organize pickup games in the neighborhood."

I told Jacob about Devin, then about Blon at the Sinclair station and how he'd taught me the reverse layup.

Jacob waggled his eyebrows.

"I saw that one. Will you teach me one day?"

I said sure.

While we talked, I studied Jacob's features. The more I looked at his nose, the more I liked its large size and unusual shape: the bump at the bridge and the way it curved downward, ever so slightly toward the tip. His lips were crimson and full, his eyelashes auburn. When he smiled, his teeth gleamed; they were big and straight, as white as piano keys. He kept jerking his head to toss his bangs out of his eyes, and I found this habit appealing. His Adam's apple was huge; it bobbed whenever he swallowed soda.

How would it feel to kiss Jacob? To rub the side of my nose against his and feel his breath warm my upper lip?

Jacob's house looked like most in Deland: wood frame with a pitched roof, a screened front porch, a picket fence, and a brick walkway leading to the front steps. Banks of azaleas, as big as station wagons, flanked each side of the house. A live oak shaded the front yard. The oak's trunk was so thick two men couldn't wrap their arms around it.

"Want to come in?" Jacob asked when we pulled to the curb.

"I can't, I'd be late for dinner. My Grandma..."

Jacob raised his eyebrows. "Some other time, then?"

On my way to Cassadaga, I kept thinking about Jacob and how much I'd enjoyed his presence. Since Eric's departure, I hadn't considered touching another boy, partly because losing Eric had been too painful; I didn't want to get hurt again. And I was still shook up by the episode at the movie theater with Peter Bohannon. If Peter had sensed my queer tendencies, it was possible others could as well. If this happened, I'd be ostracized at school; I might even get beat up.

Of course, I still touched myself in bed at night; I needed *some* form of sexual release. But the idea of getting intimate with another guy I had written off. It wouldn't lead to anything good, would it? I was better off alone, wasn't I?

Now, at home, I parked the Chevy in Grandma's driveway. The sun had set, and the hem of the western sky glowed tangerine and gold. Crickets chirped in the trees, while a swarm of fireflies sparkled above my grandma's lawn. Somewhere down the street, a dog barked.

I sat behind the steering wheel, staring through the windshield and into the depths of Grandma's cave-like garage. I thought about Jacob and how much I liked his facial features. Inside my head, I heard his laughter. Between my legs, I felt a stirring.

Careful, Tyler.

C-a-r-e-f-u-l...

CHAPTER TWENTY

oments after Thursday's dismissal bell rang, a gaggle of boys, including myself and Jacob, gathered outside the gymnasium's double doors, all of us sucking our cheeks and shifting our weight from one leg to the other, our eyes on the bulletin board. At the moment, it bore nothing but the week's cafeteria menu and a flyer announcing an upcoming school dance.

A few guys conversed, but most remained silent, just staring and blinking.

My armpits felt moist, and I couldn't stop biting my lips. I'd waited so long for this moment. I'd always felt like an outsider at school. I wasn't popular; I didn't know how to choose my clothes or get a good haircut. I couldn't dance worth a crap, and my conversational skills weren't the best. In short, I was a loser.

Making the team would boost my prestige; I'd be part of an elite group. Basketball games at our school were a big deal. Everyone went to them: students, faculty, staff, and townspeople. If I made the team, each time I'd walk onto the court in my uniform, hundreds of pairs of eyes would gaze at me. Every time I'd sink a shot, the crowd would roar. The cheerleaders would cry my name, and even Ebersole would come to respect me. I would—

Someone hissed.

"Here comes Coach," another guy whispered.

Heart pounding, I jerked my gaze toward the gymnasium doors.

Ebersole approached, crossing the hardwood court, a single sheet of paper in his paw, a blank expression on his face. He didn't even acknowledge our presence; he acted like we were invisible. Stepping to the bulletin board, his back to us, he yanked two thumbtacks from the cork. He mounted the list. Then he turned to the group and searched faces, including mine.

"For those of you who've made the cut, tomorrow morning's practice starts at six-thirty. Be on time."

He turned on his heel and strode into the gym, arms swinging, while our group rushed to the bulletin board. Every guy held his breath; each of us scanned the typewritten roster. My heart leapt into my throat. The names were listed in alphabetical order, and mine would have been first if I'd made the team, but...

My name wasn't there.

My jaw slacked, and, for a few moments, I couldn't even breathe. I felt as though the floor beneath me had disappeared and I was sinking into quicksand. I hadn't made the cut? Why?

Jacob's name was on the list, as was Mark Maggert's. Maggert swung a fist through the air. "I'm in," he cried.

All about me, boys hung their heads. They turned their backs to the bulletin board, and then shuffled off.

Charles Sweeney crowed; he jumped up and down, his face bright crimson, while Maggert slapped his back.

How I envied them, and how dismal I felt at the moment. My feet seemed heavy as concrete blocks; I couldn't seem to move them. I just stood there, staring at the list and blinking, not believing what had happened. What kind of an idiot was Ebersole? Was he blind or something? I'd outperformed at least two guys who'd made the team, I felt certain. Or *had* I? Maybe I wasn't as good as I'd thought. Maybe—

"Tyler?"

I looked at Jacob.

"I'm sorry," he said. "It's not fair."

I fought the urge to cry. My voice shook when I told Jacob, "Congratulations."

He followed me to my car, and then we climbed inside, me behind the wheel, Jacob in the passenger seat. We sat there, staring through the windshield at kids leaving school. They carried books under their arms; they laughed and chattered away, oblivious to my misery and shame.

This is what it feels like to be a failure. I'll never be a winner in life, will I?

After starting the Chevy's engine, I shifted gears and drove us from the parking lot. Neither Jacob nor I said a word, until we reached his house. After he hopped out with his books, Jacob closed the passenger door. Then he leaned his forearms on the sill and looked in at me.

"You're a good player, Ty. Maybe next year you'll, you know..."

I nodded, staring at the dashboard.

"I'll see you tomorrow," I told Jacob.

For two weeks after Ebersole cut me, I walked about school like a sleepwalker. I barely spoke to kids I knew, and found it hard to concentrate on my studies. The days dragged over me like leaden blankets, while classroom clocks seemed to move in slow motion.

At home, I lost interest in food. I moped about the house. I spent hours in my room, lying on my bed and staring at the ceiling, my mind a vacuum. I told myself I would never touch a basketball again—not ever. Already,

I had deflated both balls I owned, and I'd stowed them in a locker in Grandma's garage.

My only solace was the swimming spring. Several times, I went there with a blanket and towel. I'd get naked and bathe. Then I'd lie in the afternoon sunshine, feeling its warmth on my skin, while cicadas sang their shrill tunes. I'd think about Devin and Jesse, and the day I'd seen them make love at this spot. How long ago it seemed. I often wondered where Devin was now and what he was doing with his life. At this point, I was glad he wasn't living in Cassadaga. What disappointment he'd have felt, had he seen me fail at the sport he'd spent so much time teaching me.

The only person I communicated with was Jacob. Because he had practice twice a day—before and after school—I rarely saw him in person, unless we'd pass in the hallways at Deland High. But every evening, around eight, he'd call and tell me how things were going with Ebersole and the team.

"He's a sadist," Jacob said of Ebersole. "He works us 'til we collapse; then he works us some more. You should try running wind sprints at six-thirty in the morning. Half the time, I lose my breakfast."

Jacob reported on each player's strengths and weaknesses. I listened with perverse interest, especially when a guy who'd bested me at tryouts did something foolish and earned a tongue-lashing from Ebersole.

"Coach is always threatening to cut someone from the squad, even the seniors. He had Maggert *crying* the other day; you should've heard Ebersole chew him out: 'You're as worthless as a cat turd, Maggert, a disgrace to this team. Why don't you do us all a favor and quit? Join the marching band; play clarinet or piccolo.'"

In my mind's eye, I pictured the scene: Ebersole red-faced and barking while tears rolled down Mark

Maggert's cheeks, and the other players cowered.

Who knows? Maybe it's a blessing I got cut.

On a Friday night, when Jacob called, he said, "I can't play ball on the Sabbath; it's taboo. But why don't you come over Sunday? There's a public court near my house. My mom will fix us lunch, and then we'll play one-on-one."

"Thanks," I said, "but not this weekend."

I couldn't bear the thought of stepping onto a court, even with Jacob. My basketball days, I'd decided, were behind me.

CHAPTER TWENTY-ONE

The first week of November, a cold front swept across northeast Florida. The temperature dropped into the low forties. On Monday morning, I wore a jacket when I left the house. My breath steamed in the frigid air when I turned the key in the Chevy's ignition. Switching on the heater, I shivered; I rubbed my hands together while waiting for warm air to flow from the dashboard vents. The brightness of the sun and the sky's brilliance made me squint, so I reached for a pair of sunglasses I kept in the glove box.

At school, when I pulled into the student parking lot, an ambulance was parked near the gymnasium, its rear door ajar. I crinkled my forehead in curiosity. What was going on?

It didn't take me long to find out.

"Scheevers broke his leg," Jacob told me when I saw him in a hallway later. "He fought for a rebound, against Hartmann and Sweeney. All three guys fell, and Scheevers was at the bottom of the pile." Jacob winced and shook his head. "The bone broke clear through his skin, a really disgusting sight."

In third period English class, a student assistant from the office appeared with a blue slip addressed to me, the handwriting on it clumsy: *Buckspan, see me after dismissal. Ebersole.*

Hours later, I entered the gymnasium. Ten guys, Jacob among them, played shirts and skins; they hustled up and down the court, their sneakers squeaking on the hardwood. Ebersole stood at the court's edge, barking instructions. Mike Monroe sat in the bleachers, using a hand pump to inflate balls. The lenses of his eyeglasses reflected light from the gym's overhead lamps.

When Ebersole saw me, he jerked a thumb toward his office. In moments, we were alone behind a closed door, me standing, Ebersole seated at his desk, his big hands joined behind his head.

The cramped room was windowless, lit by fluorescent ceiling fixtures. A bookshelf held a multitude of trophies, some tarnished with age. A myriad of plaques and certificates—the latter ones displayed in cheap metal frames—decorated the room's cinder block walls, along with black–and-white photos of Ebersole posing with his uniformed teams. His desktop was littered with notebooks, writing pads, and dog-eared sports magazines.

Ebersole's gaze bore into me.

"I suppose you've heard about Scheevers?"

I nodded.

"It's a compound fracture of the tibia; he'll wear a cast two months, at least."

I lowered my gaze and didn't say anything.

"You still want to play ball for me?"

A shiver ran up to my shoulders from my feet. *Me on the team?* For a moment I thought I might wet my pants. Lifting my gaze, I opened my mouth to say something, but I couldn't think of what it should be, so I simply nodded again.

Leaning forward, Ebersole placed his elbows on his desktop. Then he formed a steeple with his fingers.

"Do you want to know why I cut you in the first place?"

Of *course* I wanted to know.

"Yes, sir," I said.

"It wasn't the quality of your play; you have talent, Buckspan. But at tryouts, every time I looked at you, you glanced away like you were scared."

Ebersole narrowed his eyes.

"I don't need bashful players on my team. Understand?"

I drew a breath. *It's a test, stupid. Keep looking him in the eye and say something.*

My knees shook and my voice quivered, but I kept my gaze fixed on Ebersole's flinty stare. I felt I was peering into an ice cave.

"Coach, I'll work hard; I promise I will. I'll work harder than anyone else on the team."

Ebersole pointed a finger.

"You'll have to, Buckspan, 'cause you've already missed three weeks of practice. Our season starts in another month; that means plenty of catch-up on your part."

"I can do it, Coach."

He raised an eyebrow.

"Be here tomorrow, at 6:30 a.m., dressed out and ready to work."

"Thanks, Coach, I—"

"Time's up, Buckspan. Now, get the hell out of here before I change my mind."

I felt like I was high on narcotics. Jolts of electricity coursed through my limbs while my lips spread into a smile as broad as a basketball hoop. While walking through the gym, I felt as though I floated above the concrete floor. I traced the court's perimeter, hearing the ball's *thunka-thunk*, and the squeak of rubber soles against hardwood. The ten players sprinted past me, and then Jacob called out my name.

"What's going on?" he cried.

I flashed him a thumbs-up.

"I made the team," I hollered.

CHAPTER TWENTY-TWO

And so I became Ebersole's indentured servant.

I'd rise before dawn and pack my gym bag with necessaries: T-shirt, gym shorts, jock strap, wool socks, Converse high-tops, and a bath towel. Caffeine helped wake me up, so I'd brew a few cups in Grandma's electric pot. Then I'd pour the steaming liquid into a thermos and take it with me in the Chevy. I'd roll down the County Road, passing farms and slash pine forests. My radio would blare numbers by The Beatles or The Yardbirds while I'd sip from my thermos. The sun would shine so brightly in the east, I'd have to wear sunglasses, just to see the road ahead of me.

Once at school, I'd join my teammates in the gymnasium's locker room. The heat wouldn't yet be turned on. We'd shiver as we undressed and slipped into our practice clothing. The smell of sweat-stained gear and mildew would be strong in the room. Few words were spoken as we did this, I think because everyone was sleepy, and also because we all knew what lay in store for us.

Each morning, first thing, Ebersole made us run wind sprints from one end of the gym to the other, back and forth, full speed, until at least two of us puked. The first guy who vomited got to clean up everyone else's mess, as well as his own.

I quickly learned to skip breakfast, sticking to coffee only.

Every morning, during practice, we did push-ups 'til our arms became rubber. Ebersole kept barbells at one corner of the gym. We used these to build up our leg strength, doing squats and calf raises until our thighs and calves burned.

Ebersole told us, "You knuckleheads think winning is all about shooting and ball handling, don't you? Well, you're wrong. Fitness is the key to success on the court; you must build your strength and stamina.

"I swear, I'll get you in the best shape of your lives; count on it. We will outrun our opponents from tip-off to final buzzer. We'll fry their lungs; their legs will *wobble* before halftime."

Mornings, after an hour of fitness training, we'd do drills: layups, dribbling, defensive maneuvers, but never any shooting practice. "Do it on your own time," Ebersole said.

Afternoons, after dismissal bell, we'd return to the locker room, change, and then run eight laps around Deland High's track. Ebersole always joined us; he'd bark at any player who wasn't keeping up with him. Then we'd hit the court for five-on-five competitions. Ebersole substituted players frequently, making sure each team member had equal time on the court. He'd march up and down the sideline, hollering instructions and blowing his whistle if something offended him.

Ebersole rarely gave compliments, but his criticisms were frequent and withering. "Numbskull" and "idiot" were epithets he often hurled when a player missed a foul shot, flubbed a rebound, or lost control of the ball while dribbling. Sometimes Coach would charge onto the court. He'd seize a player by his shoulders and shake him like a rag doll, while cursing a blue streak, right in the kid's face.

Coach tagged each player with a degrading nickname, used when Ebersole and his team members were the only persons present. Mark Maggert was "Faggert," Charles Sweeney was "Weenie," and Jacob was, of course, "Jackinoff."

Me? I was "Fuckspan."

Mostly, I played forward, a spot I preferred. I could sometimes employ my reverse layup, plus the position gave me better opportunities to rebound.

Ebersole was merciless when judging my performance on the court.

"You're a lazy piece of shit, Fuckspan; a total pussy. I don't know why I put you on the team. Get your ass in gear or, I swear, you'll join the cheerleading squad. I'll even buy your pom-poms."

Sometimes I'd ask myself, *Why do I subject myself to this guy's abuse?* But, of course, I never considered quitting. I loved being part of the team: the prestige it lent me, the thrill of competition, and the comradeship of my fellow players.

I got along well with most all my teammates, especially the juniors. Our common dislike of Ebersole's torments only cemented our brotherhood. Behind his back we called him "Asserhole," but I'll say this: Coach knew his basketball. He taught us faking techniques with our heads and shoulders, defensive maneuvers and ball-stealing tricks, all of it subtle stuff. While demonstrating, he moved quickly but delicately, like a ballerina. His ball handling was impressive; he ran circles around *any* of us when he played one-on-one with a team member. His jump shot was smooth and artistic, and I would often shake my head while watching him perform. How could a guy so bulky, a guy at least forty years old, leap so high?

Coach would not tolerate cigarette smoking.

"If I catch you *once*, you're off the team. Do you

want your body to perform? Then treat it with respect. Cigarettes are garbage, even the Surgeon General says so."

Another thing: Ebersole practiced what he preached. Mornings, when I'd arrive at the gym, Ebersole's shirt was always sweat-soaked because he'd just run five miles on the school's outdoor track. Afternoons, I'd find him doing sit-ups in the gym with his feet hooked under the first row of bleachers. His face would shine with sweat.

Seniors on our team tended to be cliquey—they treated us younger players with mild derision—so the junior players formed a sort of clan. We ate lunch in the cafeteria together. We met for pickup games on weekends. One Saturday evening, after sundown, the seven of us met at Jacob's house. Everyone piled into my Chevy, and then we visited a drive-in theater for a double feature. We guzzled Cokes and wolfed down popcorn. We told jokes and swapped gossip about kids at school.

During the movie, some guys talked about girls they'd dated or girls they *wanted* to date. They discussed the girls' bodies, and how far the girls would go in the backseat of a car. When this topic arose, I kept my mouth shut. I had no interest in women—I had no experience with them either—and I wasn't about to lie and say I did.

Mark Maggert, especially, had a reputation as a stud horse; one girl or another always clung to him in the hallways at school. A bit taller than me, with chestnut hair and dark eyes, he moved with a fluid grace I envied. When we showered after morning practice, I couldn't keep my eyes off his athletic physique; it reminded me of Devin's body, how Mark's muscles rippled under his skin. He spoke with a syrupy drawl—pronouncing my name "Tah-lah"—and he never failed to greet me when we passed each other between classes.

Of course, my favorite teammate and closest friend

was Jacob; we talked on the phone most every evening. Saturdays, after sundown, when the Jewish Sabbath ended, Jacob's dad would drop him off at my house. He'd spend the night, and we'd play one-on-one on Grandma's driveway, under the glow of the gooseneck light fixture. Our breath would steam in the chilly night air.

My bed was a three-quarter—a tight fit for both of us—and it felt nice, lying with Jacob in the darkness, feeling the warmth of his body. Both of us would wear only briefs, and our leg hairs would commingle while we talked into the wee hours.

Mornings, I'd often wake before Jacob did. I'd lie there and stare at him while sunlight burnished his hair and eyelashes, while his chest rose and fell. I'd study the peach fuzz on his upper lip and wonder how it might feel to kiss him.

It seemed as though Jacob and I never ran out of things to talk about. I'd been starved for friendship, ever since Eric's departure, and now Jacob's companionship was like a balm. We discussed current events in the paper, incidents occurring at school, popular music, Jacob's friends in Skokie, and the mischief they'd gotten into. I spoke of my days in Decatur and my deceased dad, of my grandma's psychic powers, and my trips to Daytona Beach. We talked about college and what majors we might pursue.

Jacob had an uncle named Sid, a Skokie divorce lawyer who Jacob spoke of as if his uncle were a king.

"He drives a Sedan de Ville. He lives in a split-level house with a pool and wears two hundred dollar suits, each tailor-made. He's been board chairman of Skokie's B'nai B'rith forever. Whenever a wealthy Jewish couple decides to divorce, it's a race to see who hires Sid, the husband or the wife."

Jacob said he planned to attend law school,

hopefully at University of Chicago, after completing his undergraduate studies in Florida. He hadn't decided on a Florida college as yet. Jacob's grades were as good as mine. Most all our classes were labeled "accelerated"—for studious kids only—and we both figured we'd have our pick of the state's universities.

I told him about my discussions with Peter Bohannon, omitting any mention of the theater incident.

"Peter said University of Florida and Florida State are equally good schools, but neither is easy."

Jacob said, "Maybe we should enroll at the same university. We could room together in the dorm."

The thought of sharing living quarters with Jacob made my pulse race. *Imagine, falling asleep next to Jacob each night, then waking next to him each morning.* Of course, I knew we'd occupy separate beds, but still...

Jacob and I both enjoyed reading fiction. Jacob introduced me to a Jewish writer: Isaac Bashevis Singer. Jacob lent me two of Singer's novels, *The Magician of Lublin* and *The Spinoza of Market Street*. I liked them both immensely. He also lent me a book called *Herzog*, written by a Chicago Jew named Saul Bellow, whose style I liked. Jacob and I enjoyed anything by Hemingway. Sometimes, after Jacob had spent the night with me, we'd wile away Sunday afternoon on my front porch, reading and sipping from glasses of iced tea. Both of us would sit on the glider sofa; we'd sway back and forth while turning pages.

Some things, of course, I kept from Jacob. I didn't tell him I kept a daily journal; I feared he might ask to read it. Too much personal information dwelt in the pages of those spiral notebooks. I never told Jacob of my relationship with Eric, and my discussions about Devin I kept to a minimum. I explained how Devin had stoked my interest in basketball, and how he'd taught me auto mechanics, but nothing else.

On the Saturday night following Thanksgiving, while we lay side by side in my darkened bedroom, Jacob brought up Devin's name.

"I've heard things about him—not all of them good. Are the stories true?"

My scalp prickled while I shifted my hips on the mattress.

"What have you been told?"

"People say he's a convict. They say he's homosexual, that his boyfriend killed himself when they broke up. He's also a suspect in a kidnapping and murder case."

I moistened my lips, while trying to think of the proper way to respond.

Of course he knows about these things. Folks here gossip like crazy.

I said, "He didn't kill that girl; I'm sure of it."

Jacob kept quiet a minute; then he said, "So, what's he like?"

I didn't think before answering.

"He's my half brother. He's not perfect, but I love him anyway."

Neither Jacob nor I had ever talked about girls, and I sometimes wondered if Jacob might be gay like me. I longed to ask him about it, but didn't want to risk losing his friendship. What if he reacted in a negative way?

I kept my hands to myself whenever we slept together. Jacob's friendship was a blessing, something I cherished. I loved his voice, his lanky physique, and his bumpy, freckled nose. When we lay in bed, the scents of his skin and hair enchanted me. When we showered together in the locker room, my heart thumped while I watched water sheet off his limbs. We'd chat while soaping ourselves in the steamy air, and then my gaze would slide over Jacob's frame.

Honestly, as much as Eric's physicality had thrilled me, no one had ever made my heart race like Jacob did. I longed to touch him, to hold him in my arms, and stroke his shiny hair.

We'd make perfect lovers, wouldn't we?

Of course, we came from contrasting cultures. I knew nothing of Judaism; I didn't understand its curious language and rituals, or its strange attires.

Once, we visited the Rexall pharmacy Jacob's father operated in Deland. Jacob had introduced me to his dad, a man as tall as Jacob, with a rust-red beard. He wore a tasseled, cloth belt and a circular cap that looked like it was made of silk. When he spoke, his English was flavored with an accent—Russian I later found out. As a boy, he'd immigrated to the States in the 1930s, along with his parents.

"The cap's called a *yarmulke*," Jacob told me, when I asked about the clothing his dad had worn. "On Saturdays, I wear one to temple. The tasseled thing around Dad's waist is a prayer belt; we call it a *gartel*."

When I told Jacob about Grandma's occupation, and about my personal experiences with spirituality, he looked at me like I was nuts. I couldn't blame him, really. Cassadaga was a freakish place full of weird people who harbored unorthodox beliefs. I was hardly in a position to view Jacob's religion as strange.

Aside from our talk about Devin, homosexuality came up in our conversation only one other time, when Jacob told me about his gay uncle named Isaac.

"He's a handsome guy with a great singing voice. He performs in musicals, up in Chicago, and my family never misses his shows. Ever seen *South Pacific*?"

I shook my head.

"Isaac played the part of Lieutenant Cable. His character falls in love with a Polynesian girl—a daring thing to do in the 1940s."

I wondered how his family would feel about *us* falling in love, but dared not ask the question. Showering next to Jacob, and sleeping beside him, would be as far as things between us would go.

And that was enough, right?

CHAPTER TWENTY-THREE

Our opening game of the 1965–66 season, we played at home. Our opponent was Mainland High School from Daytona Beach. By then, I'd gained six pounds—all of it leg muscle. I could run two miles around Deland High's track in thirteen minutes.

In the pregame locker room, I felt like a kid at Christmas when I slipped into my satin uniform. My forest-green jersey and shorts featured white lettering and stripes on the flanks. My player number was ten. I wore a new pair of canvas, high-top sneakers I'd bought with money I'd earned at the Sinclair station, and striped knee socks.

Ebersole had us form a circle in the locker room. Each player held hands with the guys to the left and right of him. Ebersole stood in the middle. He spoke to us in a tone far gentler than normal; it almost sounded like he was saying grace before dinner. Gone were the bark, the snarl, the derisive sneer, and insulting nicknames.

"I know I've been harsh on you guys, demanding too. It's because I wanted each of you—even our latecomer, Buckspan—to be the best you possibly could. I'm proud to say you've all risen to the challenge. You're fit and well-trained. Believe me, you can beat these guys—you'll run them right out of the gym—but only if you have the will and the desire to do so. I can't win this game for us; my work's done. I'll be on the sidelines and nearly helpless.

"*You* must win this victory. In order to do so, each of you must make a commitment to yourself and your teammates. Each of you must tell yourself, 'This is what I've worked for.' This is what everyone in this room has worked for. Not just in recent weeks, but ever since the first of us picked up a basketball, as a child."

Ebersole pointed a finger at the ceiling.

"Don't let me down, gentlemen. Win this game for me, for your school and your families, and, most of all, for yourselves. Concentrate on the fundamentals: ball handling, setting up shots, and lay-ups. No fancy stuff. I want *dogged* defense: full-court press the entire game. Make these guys sorry they ever walked onto our campus; send them home exhausted and whipped."

A preacher from Deland's First Baptist—an old guy in a white shirt and tie, with a widow's peak and skin as pale as cake flour—said a prayer while everyone bowed their heads. The preacher intoned Jesus' name, referring to him as "Christ our Savior," and I wondered how Jacob must feel, being forced to participate in something he didn't believe in.

When we trotted onto the gymnasium floor, the Deland High marching band, seated in the bleachers, played the Florida Gators' fight song. A crowd of eight hundred rose to their feet, hollering and clapping their hands so loud I swear the building shook. A shiver ran through me while I scanned the spectators. When I spotted my mom and Grandma, I waved to them. Cletis Hyde and Blon O'Keefe, both wearing their Sinclair uniforms, were there as well. Mike Scheevers, his leg still in a cast, sat behind our bench.

The players from Daytona's Mainland High School were all bigger than Hartmann—our tallest player—and

I wondered if Ebersole had really believed what he'd said in the locker room. Could we beat these guys?

It seemed so.

Halfway through the first quarter, we'd already stolen the ball from Mainland five times, and we'd outscored them sixteen to seven. The guys from Daytona were simply too slow. Our full-court press flustered them, and despite their height advantage, we continually out-rebounded them. Ebersole's weight training had paid off: our guys jumped like crickets; they plucked the ball from the backboard, and then sent it screaming down the court.

I spent the game's first half on the bench, as did Jacob and all the other juniors except Mark Maggert, who played in Scheever's stead. I itched to appear on the court, to show my teammates, my family, and everyone else just how committed I was to winning.

In the locker room during half time, Ebersole paced the concrete floor while my teammates and I sat on benches. The seniors and Maggert toweled their sweaty skins, drank water from paper cups. Their jerseys stuck to their torsos. We held a 36–17 lead, and every face in the room was afire. Our first string had performed as smoothly as a Porsche's engine.

"We've got them on the run," Ebersole said. "Their legs are already rubber. But don't get overconfident. In basketball, a nineteen-point lead can vanish quicker than a rainbow. You must stay focused. Keep up the full-court press; it's driving them nuts. I can see it in their faces."

By third quarter's end, the score was 52–28. The crowd, mostly Deland supporters, roared every time we stole the ball or scored points. By now, all of Mainland's first string had left the game. They sat on their bench, their shoulders sagging, their forearms resting on their knees, heads hanging. Mainland's coach, a skinny, hatchet-faced man with thinning hair, seemed on the verge of apoplexy.

His complexion was brick-red and shiny. He paced the sideline, twisting a spiral notebook in his fists; he shouted at his players. The armpits of his dress shirt were damp, and his necktie was askew.

Ebersole called a time-out. He squatted, while our team gathered around him, our hands on our knees. Each player's gaze was fixed on Ebersole.

"I'm taking the first string out," he said. "You guys need a rest."

Ebersole ordered five juniors onto the court, me and Jacob included. I was assigned forward, as was Jacob. My heart thumped in my chest; for a moment I feared I might hyperventilate. I had dreamed of this moment for so long. Was I up to the task?

Calm down, Tyler. Concentrate.

Mainland's second stringers were all bigger than us, but like their first-string teammates, they were slow. Their ball handling wasn't too agile, and our full-court press confused them. They kept trying to set up shots, but we wouldn't let them. Twice I stole the ball from a kid I'd been assigned to defend, a lumbering giant with a shock of red hair and legs like tree trunks.

We scored thirteen points during the fourth quarter, three of them mine. I sank a jump shot, a beauty that swished through the net. Just after I released the ball, the red-haired kid slammed into me, and knocked me to the court. When I made my free throw, moments later, the crowd went crazy and a shiver ran through me.

This is what victory feels like.

The final score was 65–35.

In the locker room, Ebersole was strangely subdued. All he said was, "Good game, gentlemen. Now hit the showers."

By the time I'd dressed and packed up my gym bag, Ebersole had disappeared into his office and closed the door.

In the school's parking lot, Jacob and I stood beside the Chevy, discussing the game and our own, personal performances. The night air was crisp, the moon was up, and a multitude of stars dotted the sable sky. Beams from headlights swept over us while cars left the lot. I felt exhilarated, so keyed up I couldn't stand still. I wanted to seize Jacob by his shoulders. I wanted to pull him to me, to kiss his lips, and slip my tongue inside his mouth.

Wouldn't it be a great way to celebrate our win?

But how would he react?

We both wore letterman's sweaters, forest green with white numbers and letters, and the Deland High Bulldogs mascot above the breast pockets. Jacob looked regal in his, I thought, and I felt proud to wear mine.

I thought of Devin and wondered how he might feel, if he could see me now. I was his basketball protégé, now turned victor. I thought of the first day we'd played one-on-one, and how awkwardly I'd performed. Under Devin's patient tutelage, I had learned so much on Grandma's driveway.

I pictured Devin in my mind's eye, recalling the first time we'd visited the spring. I thought of his emerald eyes, his smooth skin and rippling muscles, his velvety baritone voice.

Oh, Devin, how I miss you.

Another pair of headlight beams passed over us, and their brightness snapped me from my reverie. The light reflected in Jacob's eyes, in his teeth when his lips parted. I studied his lanky frame, recalling how sexy he'd looked, minutes before in the locker room showers, the water streaming off him.

Did he ever think about me in a sexual way? Who knew?

"Got plans for Saturday night?" he asked.

I shook my head.

"Mind if I sleep over?"
My belly fluttered.
"That'd be great," I said.

CHAPTER TWENTY-FOUR

After months of cajoling, my mom had finally convinced Grandma a television would not poison our home. Now, a black-and-white console, as big as Grandma's cookstove, with knobs the size of hockey pucks, occupied one corner of our living room, purchased by Mom with her beauty shop earnings. And despite Grandma's declaration that she'd *never* watch the thing, I often found her seated in her new Barcalounger, with her legs crossed at the ankles on the raised footstool, and her gaze fixed on the flickering screen. She particularly liked movies shown after the eleven o'clock news.

On the Saturday night following our contest with Mainland High, after Jacob and I finished our one-on-one contest, we found Grandma in her robe and slippers, watching Alfred Hitchcock's *Vertigo*. Our sweatshirts were damp; they clung to our chests.

Grandma looked at us and sniffed the air. Then she shook her head. "You boys need a shower."

My mom was in St. Augustine for the weekend, staying with relatives, so Jacob and I had upstairs to ourselves, for the moment at least. We took turns showering; then we lounged about my bedroom with the door closed, wearing only our briefs. We thumbed through back issues of *Sports Illustrated*. We talked about school, about the Mainland game and, most of all, about Ebersole's transformation from tyrant to inspirational speaker.

"Was all that yelling and name-calling just an act?" Jacob said. "Do you think, deep down, he's a nice guy?"

I stole glances at the bulge between Jacob's thighs while I told him what I'd overheard Hartmann say in the locker room, right after the Mainland game. "Hartmann told Maggert, 'Last year I hated Ebersole—at first, anyway. Then, just before our first game, he spoke to us like he did here tonight, and I realized he wasn't really an asshole. I love Coach now. He cares for us more than he ever lets on.'"

Jacob shook his head while a smile crept across his face.

Around midnight, we killed the bedroom lights. We crawled under the covers, and our shoulders and hips touched. Jacob's leg hairs tickled mine. I smelled the soap he'd bathed with earlier. The scent of his hair reminded me of freshly mown grass. He crossed his arms at his chest and closed his eyes.

"Good night, Tyler."

"Sleep well, Jacob."

I closed my eyes, and soon drifted into sleep.

I woke to the sound of Jacob's voice. He wasn't in bed any longer. He stood near a window, staring through the pane, his hands hanging at his hips, his fingers flexing. Moonlight gave his pale skin a ghostly appearance. He spoke in a language I didn't recognize, and his voice trembled as he cried out. He pointed at something or someone I could not see.

I glanced at my alarm clock's illuminated face.

It's 3:00 a.m.

"Jacob," I whispered, "what's going on?"

He didn't respond; instead he kept on pointing and crying out.

Rubbing my eyes with my knuckles, I rose in the chilly room. Goose bumps popped up on my arms and legs. I shuffled across the prickly carpet, placed a hand on Jacob's shoulder. I spoke his name, but he didn't seem to hear me; he kept on babbling.

I raised my voice and shook his shoulder.

"Jacob, what the heck are you doing?"

Flinching, he jerked his head and looked at me. Then his gaze traveled about the room, as if he didn't know where he was. He looked like a child lost in a department store.

"Come to bed," I told him.

Under the covers, we spoke in whispers. Jacob lay on his back with his arms folded behind his head. I lay on my side and facing Jacob, my elbow bent, my head resting on the heel of my hand. Moonlight allowed me to see Jacob clearly: his eyes and eyelashes, and his shiny hair.

His voice trembled while he spoke.

"I'm a sleepwalker; I always have been. Sometimes my parents will find me in the yard—in the middle of the night—talking to a tree or a shrub."

Jacob moistened his lips.

"I just had the strangest dream: I was in the army—not here but in Israel. I fired a machine gun; it sat on a tripod. I killed soldiers; I don't know who they were, but I could see them fall when I shot them."

When I asked what language he'd spoken in his sleep, he said, "Hebrew, I'm sure."

I placed a hand on Jacob's shoulder. He trembled so badly the bed shook. I said, "You're frightened, aren't you?"

He nodded.

"It was scary watching men die and knowing I might die too."

"But it was only a dream, and now it's over."

I turned onto my back and stared at the ceiling. We lay in silence a few minutes. Jacob's breath whistled in his nose. His trembling continued, and I wondered if he might hyperventilate.

"Tyler, if I turn on my side, will you hold me 'til I calm down?"

My heart skipped a beat.

"Sure," I said.

The sheets and blanket rustled, as Jacob turned away from me. I draped an arm across his chest and pulled him to me. My pectorals met his shoulder blades, my hips pressed against his buttocks, and I felt a stirring in my groin. Physically, this was as close as I'd ever been to Jacob. His skin felt warm and smooth.

Don't get stiff. Don't ...

I counted to twenty inside my head while Jacob drew a breath, and then let it out. He spoke to me in a whisper.

"Tyler?"

"Yeah?"

"Thanks for being my friend."

My eyes itched and my nose filled up with snot.

I cleared my throat.

"You're welcome, Jacob," was the best I could manage to say.

CHAPTER TWENTY-FIVE

The Monday following the Mainlands game, I entered Deland High's gymnasium at quarter past six in the morning.

Jacob was already in the locker room, changing into his practice clothing. When I looked at him, I recalled waking next to him, the previous morning, in my room. My arm had still been draped across around his chest. The tip of my nose was buried in his hair, and my hips rested against his buttocks.

Now, just thinking about it made my crotch tingle.

I undressed while Jacob laced his sneakers. Other team members filed in, their eyes swollen from sleep, voices croaky, and cowlicks standing up from the crowns of their heads like apostrophes. No one said much; the exhilaration we'd all enjoyed after our victory was gone now, replaced by sober anticipation of this morning's practice session.

Ebersole burst from his office, his T-shirt damp in the armpits, his hair matted.

"Fuckspan," he hollered.

Then he tossed me the keys to our locker room closet.

"Monroe's home with the flu. Fetch a dozen balls and take them to the court."

Ebersole pointed at Jacob.

"Find the air pump, Jackinoff; make sure every ball's properly inflated. *Move* it, you two numbskulls."

While Ebersole stormed from the room, Jacob and I looked at each other and rolled our eyes. Over in a corner, Hartmann grinned and shook his head. As soon as Coach was out of earshot, Hartmann sang to us in falsetto.

"*Asserhole*'s back, girls."

Indeed he was. Six guys puked during wind sprints, including me. We worked our legs with barbells until our muscles ached, until they felt like hot coals burning beneath our skins. We ran drills, double time, while Ebersole barked and taunted us.

"Fuckspan, you're slower than molasses in January. Pick up the pace or, I swear, I'll jam a broom handle up your lazy ass."

When we hit the showers, my legs wobbled so badly I feared I might fall down. I stood under a nozzle. The air about me steamed. Jacob joined me and soaped his limbs, but I felt so tired I couldn't even *think* about sex.

Jacob looked at me and worked his jaw.

"So much for 'Coach Nice Guy,' huh?"

I couldn't help myself.

I laughed until my eyes crossed.

By Christmas break, we'd won six games and lost only one—to Boone High School in Orlando. The Boone team had had three black guys on their first string—all of them huge. Their fluid style of play baffled us. They weren't the least bit intimidated by our full-court press; they simply dodged past us. They passed the ball back and forth, moving so quickly I could barely keep my eye on the ball. They sank twenty-five-foot jump shots as easily as free throws.

Two of our starters fouled out before half time.

When Ebersole put me in the game, the guy he assigned me to defend kept blowing past me as if I weren't there.

The final score was 68–40. In the locker room afterward, a couple of guys wept and we all hung our heads. We had tasted defeat for the first time.

Ebersole did his best to console us.

"We got beat by a better team, and there's no shame in that. I don't care how fit we are, or how much we practice, there will always be squads better than us. Boone has two thousand students—three times our enrollment. You fellows did your best, and that's all I can ask from you. Grab a shower, now. Then let's climb on the bus and go home."

On a Saturday in mid-December, I Christmas-shopped in Deland, at stores on New York Avenue. I bought Grandma a new robe, Mom a small bottle of Chanel No. 5. Afterward, while I walked down the sidewalk with my purchases, I saw a familiar sight: Byron Teague's Fleetwood, with its Confederate flag license plate; it hulked before Mr. Rachinoff's drug store. Sunlight glanced off the Fleetwood's massive chrome grille and front bumper and off the windshield I'd cleaned so many times.

Above the drug store's alcove entrance, the orange-and-blue Rexall sign gleamed.

I stood at a corner, waiting for the light to change so I could cross the street, and wondering what Teague was up to. It had been months since I'd last seen him.

Teague and Jacob's dad emerged from the Rexall. Teague led with his arms chugging, his chin lowered, and his ever-present fedora perched on his head.

Mr. Rachinoff wore his prayer belt and yarmulke.

His beard was a splash of color against the drabness of New York Avenue's brown brick storefronts. He spoke to Teague, but Teague kept his back turned to Mr. Rachinoff, until Teague reached the Fleetwood. Teague turned to Jacob's dad; he pointed a finger, and then said something I couldn't hear.

Teague's face was flushed. While he spoke, Mr. Rachinoff listened; he tugged at his beard, and he did not say anything back.

Teague shook a fist in Mr. Rachinoff's face. Then he climbed into the Fleetwood and slammed the door. The Fleetwood's engine roared to life. When Teague pulled from the curb, his tires squealed, and then the Fleetwood's rear wheels fishtailed.

While I watched the Fleetwood careen down New York Avenue, I thought of my conversation the previous summer with Cletis, in the bay at the Sinclair station. What was it he'd said about Byron Teague?

He's not someone you want as an enemy.

Now, the memory made me shudder.

CHAPTER TWENTY-SIX

The second week of January, just after Deland High's dismissal bell rang, I walked toward afternoon basketball practice with a stack of books under my arm. I heard shouting; it came from behind the gymnasium.

"You fucking kike. You chickenshit sheenie."

A crowd of students, mostly guys, had gathered, forming a semicircle. Inside it, Butch Delay, the ruffian from Deland's infamous redneck clan, had backed Jacob up against the gym's cinder block wall; Butch used both hands to shove Jacob in his chest. Jacob's books lay scattered on the asphalt. His face was crimson, his eyes bugged. When I drew closer, Butch slapped Jacob's cheek.

Jacob's head jerked from the blow.

"What's the matter, Jew Boy? Don't they teach you how to fight in Kike Country?"

I'd never been in a fistfight in my life—I knew nothing about combat—and I was certain Jacob didn't either. Despite the fact Jacob was taller than Butch, I knew Jacob wouldn't stand a chance if he tried defending himself, not if I didn't help him.

Hurry up, Tyler.

After setting my books down, I felt my heart bang against my rib cage while I pushed my way through the crowd. I approached Butch from behind. My gaze met Jacob's. I drew a breath, and then I rushed at Butch, tackling him at the waist and driving him to the asphalt, facedown.

Behind me, someone hooted while Butch squirmed beneath me, cursing. He turned onto his back and looked into my eyes. A grin spread across his pimply face when he saw it was me. His breath smelled like peanut butter and pickles.

"Goddamn Buckspan," Butch said. He shook his head while his chest rose and fell.

"What're you, some kind of Jew-lover?"

I felt Butch's muscles tense. Then he pushed me off him like I was a rag doll. I fell onto my back, while kids in the crowd hollered. Butch rose. When I tried to get up, he kicked me in the stomach and knocked the breath out of me. I fell onto my back again. I looked at the sky, at passing clouds, while Butch towered over me, his fists at his hips.

"Come on, faggot, get up and fight."

"Butch, look out," a boy hollered.

I rose onto my elbows. Swinging my gaze, I watched as Jacob tried tackling Butch, like I had moments before. Sadly, Butch turned in time to see Jacob lunge at him. Butch sidestepped the tackle, and Jacob tumbled to the asphalt with a thud. His elbows bled. One knee of his chinos was ripped. Butch kicked Jacob in his chest; Jacob fell onto his back. Then Butch kicked Jacob's ribs—hard.

Jacob cried out, while the crowd of kids gasped.

We're screwed. Butch will beat us bloody.

I never found out where Ebersole came from, or how he'd learned of the fight. But suddenly he was present. After approaching Butch from behind, Ebersole wrapped an elbow around Butch's throat. Coach seized Butch's arm; he bent the arm behind Butch's back.

Butch howled in pain.

Ebersole looked like he was high on some exotic drug. His eyes gleamed, and his lips drew back from his teeth in a malicious grin. Ebersole's bulk made Butch look like a seventh grader. Butch didn't even *try* to defend himself, or to break Ebersole's grip.

Ebersole brought his lips to Butch's ear. Then Coach spoke to Butch loudly enough so everyone present would hear.

"You ignorant redneck. You stinking, low-class hillbilly; I ought to break your arm—right here, right now."

Ebersole applied pressure to Butch's arm.

Butch squealed; his face was as red as a ripe tomato, and shiny with sweat. Saliva drooled from one corner of his gaping mouth.

Coach continued.

"DeLay, I'm only going to tell you this once. When you get home, share this information with your redneck, piece-of-shit father. If I ever catch you *near* one of my players again, whether it's Rachinoff or Buckpsan or anyone else, I'll come out to that garbage dump your family calls a house. Then I'll stomp your old man's worthless ass into next week. Got it?"

When Butch didn't respond, Ebersole wrenched Butch's arm.

Butch screamed. The sound echoed off the gymnasium wall.

"I asked you a question, *boy*."

Butch babbled while tears rolled down his cheeks.

"I got it, Coach; I heard you loud and clear."

By now, Jacob and I were on our feet and brushing dirt from our clothing. Jacob examined his bloody elbows. All around us, kids stared.

Ebersole released Butch; he shoved Butch to his knees.

Butch toppled onto his side; he clutched the arm Ebersole had twisted. Butch rocked back and forth on the asphalt. He groaned and whimpered like a whipped dog.

Ebersole let his gaze travel through the faces in the crowd. His expression was grim, and his gray eyes glared under his bushy brows.

"What I just told DeLay applies to anyone else at this school: touch one of my players and—I swear to God— I'll make you wish you'd never drawn breath. Have I made myself clear?"

A chorus of male voices responded.

"Yes, Coach."

Ebersole looked at me and Jacob. He spoke to us in a matter-of-fact tone, like we'd just passed an hour together in an ice cream parlor.

"Gather your books, gentlemen. You're tardy for practice."

Fifteen minutes later, Jacob and I jogged on Deland High's cinder track. Bandages adorned Jacob's elbows.

I asked him, "What happened? How'd the fight start?"

He raised his shoulders and shook his head. "I walked to practice, minding my own business, when Butch came up and got in my face. He said something like, 'Is that Jew who runs the Rexall store your old man?' When I said yes, Butch said, 'He looks like an ape in a woman's apron. Is he a fag or something?'"

Holy crap.

"Next thing I knew, Butch had me cornered behind the gym. He would've beaten the shit out of me, if you hadn't come along."

"I wasn't much help," I said. "Ebersole saved our butts."

We jogged in silence for a bit. Then I asked Jacob, "Why's Butch angry at you?"

Jacob shook his head. "I guess Butch doesn't like Jews."

After practice, I drove to the Sinclair station. A chilly breeze blew a soda can across the station's concrete apron, while I pumped my own gas. The dials on the pump spun; a bell ding-dinged each time another gallon gushed into the Chevy's tank. At the time, gas cost eighteen cents per gallon, so my fill-up cost nearly four dollars—a half-day's pay for me.

Blon was in the lube bay, servicing a Chrysler New Yorker. In the second bay, Cletis leaned over the fender of a shiny Oldsmobile 98. The car's hood was raised, and Cletis looked much like the circus guy who sticks his head inside a lion's mouth.

Bessie occupied the office; she made entries in her ledger book. After I paid her for my gas, I greeted Blon. He drained dirty oil from the New Yorker's engine, into a metal collection vessel.

"You're a lot sharper on the court these days," Blon told me, "and quicker too. Ebersole must be a good coach."

I said I had to agree.

I ambled into Cletis' bay, inhaling familiar scents: kerosene, grease, rubber, and cigarette smoke. Cletis installed new spark plugs in the Olds. When saw me, he extended an arm.

"Hand me a socket wrench, Ty—three-eighths, please."

I found the wrench and gave it to Cletis. Then I watched while he used a gauge to gap a spark plug, before inserting the plug into the Oldsmobile's engine block. The wrench made a whizzing sound when he twisted it.

Cletis sang in his gravely baritone.

"There was an old farmer named Fritz, who planted ten acres of tits. And then in the fall—red nipples and all—he chewed 'em and sucked 'em to bits."

While Cletis gapped another spark plug, I rested my forearms on the Oldsmobile's fender.

I asked Cletis, "What do you know about the DeLay family?"

Cletis shook his head. Raising his upper lip, he displayed his yellowed central incisors.

"They're white trash, the whole lot of 'em. Dumb as fence posts too. I went to school with the old man, Cecil. He never bathed; always stank like a skunk. And he couldn't do long division or spell worth a shit."

Cletis reached into his shirt pocket and fished out a Chesterfield. After lighting up, he shook his match and looked at me.

"What's your interest in those varmints?"

I told Cletis about Butch, and the fight he'd started that day.

I said, "Does his family hate Jews?"

Cletis blew a stream of smoke.

"They hate *everybody*: Jews, Negroes, Cubans, you name it. They're the kind of folks who think they build themselves up, when they tear other folks down. Know what I mean?"

I nodded. "Do you think they're involved with the Klan?"

Cletis squinted. "How come you're asking?"

I told Cletis about Byron Teague's confrontation with Jacob's dad, in front of the Rexall.

"Teague was angry," I said.

Cletis rubbed his jaw with the heel of his hand. He drew on his cigarette while his gaze darted here and there. Lowering his voice, he told me, "I've no doubt Cecil's Ku

Klux. He'd fit right in with those knuckleheads."

I pulled at my fingers, while I shifted my weight from one leg to the other.

"Is Mr. Rachinoff in trouble?"

Cletis raised a shoulder.

"I can't say, Ty; I really can't. But I told you before: a guy shouldn't get on Teague's bad side. It's inviting mischief."

CHAPTER TWENTY-SEVEN

At my request, Mom and Grandma had given me a canvas tent and two sleeping bags for Christmas. And on the last Saturday night in January, after sundown when Jewish Sabbath ended, Jacob came to my house. Then we camped on the banks of the spring.

Blon had bought me a six-pack of beer, and now the cans floated in the water. Pine boughs crackled and hissed in the fire pit, while sparks rose into the night sky. The smell of smoke and the stars' brightness reminded me of many nights I'd spent at the spring with Eric. Because the air was cool, Jacob and I wore bomber-style jackets, with elastic cuffs and waistbands.

Earlier, after we'd pitched the tent, I opened both sleeping bags all the way, so they lay flat, one on top of the other.

"I've never camped," Jacob said while watching me. "Why aren't we sleeping in separate bags?"

My scalp prickled. *Finesse this, Tyler.*

"It's more comfortable this way, less confining."

Jacob shrugged and didn't say anything.

At the fire pit's edge, we sat on a carpet of pine needles, sipping from beer cans and eating potato chips. A three-quarter moon crested the treetops; its silvery light reflected in the spring's surface. I'd only drunk beer a few times before—the same was true of Jacob—and after we'd each consumed two cans, we grew silly. We cracked jokes and giggled like a pair of schoolgirls.

Every time I looked at Jacob, I thrilled at the way his hazel eyes reflected firelight, and the way his teeth gleamed when he smiled. He kept tossing his bangs from his forehead, and licking the corners of his mouth. I studied his freckled nose, his full lips, and the stubble growing on his chin—a little patch of whiskers barely visible. My groin tingled at these sights.

I felt nervous as a cat.

Already, I had decided I would make a pass at Jacob tonight. Our location was remote and isolated. However things went, the outcome would be known only to us. I'd pondered this overture ever since the night Jacob had sleepwalked in my room, and he'd asked me to hold him in bed. He had seemed perfectly at ease with our closeness. Now, when I thought of how it felt to rest my hips against Jacob's buttocks, my pulse quickened.

It had been a year and a half since I'd last touched Eric, and I was starved for physical affection from another boy. My desire for Jacob ran deep, not just because he was handsome, but because I truly cared for him. He was my best friend, my teammate, and my constant companion. We never quarreled, and our shared interests made everything easy.

I asked myself for the twentieth time that night, *Am I putting our friendship at risk?*

Over and over I'd told myself the potential for our happiness was worth taking the chance. At worst, Jacob would reject my advances. He'd say, "Cut it out, Ty," and things would go on as before. But maybe—just maybe—we'd become lovers. And how wonderful would *that* be? I could hold Jacob in my arms as I'd once held Eric. We would make love in discreet places, sharing our deepest needs and feelings.

My pulse raced as I looked at Jacob in the firelight. How would it feel to stroke his cheek with a fingertip, to kiss the bump on his freckly nose?

Around midnight, when the beer was finished, we peed into a blackberry bush, side by side. Then we crawled inside the tent and got undressed. We wore only T-shirts and briefs. The temperature had dropped, and our breaths steamed in the frigid air. We shivered between the sleeping bags.

"My teeth are chattering," Jacob said.

There's your opening.

"Turn onto your side," I told him, "and we'll warm each other up."

Jacob did so, and then I draped my arm across his chest. I pulled him to me, like I had the night he had sleepwalked in my bedroom. His legs made contact with my legs, and the hair on his calves tickled mine. Jacob's skin felt warm and inviting. We lay like that a few minutes, our chests rising and falling. Then I brought my face to the back of Jacob's head. I buried the tip of my nose in his hair, inhaling its grassy scent.

Jacob cleared his throat and shifted his hips.

I kissed Jacob behind his ear while my hand traveled from his chest to the hem of his T-shirt. After lifting the hem, I made circles on his belly with my palm.

Jacob shuddered. He seized my hand; then he moved it south, in between his thighs.

It's happening...

Already, Jacob was stiff.

In the hour that followed, I tasted every part of Jacob's body, and he reciprocated. His lovemaking was tender and generous; it thrilled me to no end. His hair was soft as corn silk, his skin as smooth and white as porcelain. He kissed like a dream; I couldn't get enough of him. My heart thumped so hard I thought it might burst from my body.

I didn't ask Jacob how he'd acquired his knowledge of male-male lovemaking. Perhaps from his gay uncle? But I didn't even care. Wasn't it enough he shared himself with me now?

Afterward, Jacob told me, "That was amazing." His head lay on my chest, and I stroked his hair, feeling a sense of wonderment.

He's your boyfriend now. It's like a miracle...

I woke in the tent, to the sound of birds tweeting in the slash pines.

I was alone.

After sitting up, I pulled aside a flap and peaked out, squinting at the brightness of the morning. I expected to see Jacob peeing into a bush or washing his face in the spring, but he wasn't there. His clothes were gone too.

I called Jacob's name, two or three times.

No answer.

What was going on?

Back at Grandma's, I phoned Jacob's house. When his mother answered, I asked if Jacob were home.

"He is," Mrs. Rachinoff told me, "but he's not feeling well; his stomach's upset. He's in bed right now."

I stood beside Grandma's telephone stand, rubbing the pad of my thumb with an index finger. I felt an urge to drive the Chevy to Jacob's home, to confront him and find out why he'd left me alone at the spring, but I didn't. Already, a dreadful question dwelt inside my head. Had I just ruined my friendship with Jacob? Did he feel as I had felt in the movie theater with Peter Bohannon: ambushed and played for a fool?

Jacob's behavior bewildered me. What was he thinking right now? Was he angry? Confused? Frightened? Did he feel I'd taken advantage of him?

I said to Mrs. Rachinoff, "Please tell Jacob I hope he feels better, that I'll see him at practice tomorrow morning."

"All right, Tyler. I will."

I hung up the phone and stared out a window. Then I worked my jaw from side to side.

Numbskull, I think maybe you screwed up.

Monday morning, Jacob was already dressed out and practicing his jump shot when I entered the gymnasium, toting my canvas bag. When he saw me, I waved to him and he raised a palm, but he didn't smile or say anything. He kept on dribbling and making shots while I entered the locker room to change. Several guys were present, all sleepy-eyed. Through his open office door, I saw Ebersole converse with Monroe. Coach sat on the edge of his desktop, twirling a ball on the tip of his index finger, while Monroe took notes on a clipboard.

The locker room's usual scents—mildew, damp cloth, rubber, and sweat—made my stomach churn. I wanted to bolt from the room, to charge across the court and confront Jacob, but of course I couldn't.

During wind sprints, I was the first to puke. After two more guys vomited, I had the honor of cleaning up the mess. On my hands and knees, I mopped up sticky liquid, along with chunks of ham, eggs, and biscuits. My nose crinkled at the rancid aroma. I kept looking at Jacob, but he wouldn't look at me while the team formed lay-up lines, and then guys took turns charging the goal.

Jacob didn't even speak to me when we showered after practice. He waited until I chose a nozzle. Then he used one at the opposite end of the tiled room, keeping his gaze low and soaping his limbs. I studied his body, recalling how I'd touched him at the spring Saturday night, and my heart ached to do it again.

I felt miserable and panicky; I was going nuts.

After dressing hastily, I left the locker room before Jacob did. Then I stationed myself outside the gymnasium's double doors. When Jacob emerged, he saw me and looked away, as if I weren't there. He didn't even break his stride.

"Jacob," I cried, "wait up."

He stopped in the hallway and I approached him. He looked so handsome in his letter sweater, white shirt, pressed chinos, and penny loafers. Morning sunlight burnished his hair. All around us, kids hustled toward classes, the guys with notebooks and texts under their arms, the girls clutching books to their breasts.

"What's going on?" I asked Jacob. "Why are you avoiding me?"

He looked at something over my shoulder.

"Tell me what's wrong?" I said.

He swung his gaze to me, and his cheeks colored.

"I think you know," he said.

My voice sounded funny when I spoke.

"Can we talk about it?"

He glanced here and there. "Not right now."

"After practice this afternoon?"

He rubbed the tip of his nose, not looking at me.

"Jacob, don't shut me out. Please, meet me at my car after practice."

Jacob looked at me and nodded. Then he looked away.

"All right, Tyler," was all he said.

We sat in the Chevy, in the school's empty parking lot.

Already, the sun had dipped behind the western tree line. Light drained from the sky. Jacob sat on the passenger side, his books resting in his lap. He kept his gaze fixed on the windshield, while he fingered the corner of a text cover.

"What we did was wrong," he said.

"Why? Didn't you enjoy it?"

He glanced at me. Then he returned his gaze to the windshield.

"Of course," he said, "but that doesn't make it okay. It's a sin in the eyes of God." He shifted his weight in the car seat. "And what if someone found out? What then?"

"Jacob, I won't tell anyone. This can be something private between us." I told Jacob about Eric and me, at length, all the details. "No one ever suspected, I'm sure. It could be the same for us, if you'll let it happen."

Jacob looked at me and shook his head.

"You don't understand; I can't be your boyfriend. Don't think for a *minute* I can be. I have obligations to God and my family. I'm my parents' only son; I have a duty to give them grandchildren."

"What about your uncle? The actor in Chicago you told me about?"

"You mean Isaac?"

I nodded.

"That's different: he's not an Orthodox Jew. Plus, he comes from a large family; he has four brothers."

Already, I could see I'd get nowhere if I tried convincing Jacob he was wrong.

"Are we still friends?" I asked.

He stared at the books in his lap.

"I guess," he said. Then he looked at me. "But we can't touch each other—not in that way—ever again. Understand?"

I wanted to cry. I felt like someone had cut out my

heart and tossed it to a wolf. My stomach churned while I swung my gaze to the windshield. How could things have gone so wrong, so fast?

Voice quivering, I told Jacob, "If that's how you want it, okay. I won't touch you again—not like that—I promise."

Jacob declined my offer of a ride home.

Watching him walk across the parking lot, I shook my head.

Shit...

CHAPTER TWENTY-EIGHT

On a Saturday afternoon in mid-February, I descended the stairs in Grandma's house, my basketball under an arm. I whistled a tune, "I Wanna Hold Your Hand" by the Beatles, as I entered the kitchen. I planned to pour myself a glass of milk, but then I froze when I saw my grandma.

She lay on the linoleum floor in her housedress, her face pale, her mouth agape. Her glasses were askew, a shoe had fallen from one foot, and her eyes were closed.

After dropping to my knees beside her, I shook her shoulder. "Grandma, what's wrong?"

No response.

Her chest rose and fell; she was alive, but I knew something was seriously wrong. I called the fire department first, Mom second. For twenty minutes, I sat beside Grandma on the kitchen floor, holding her hand and saying whatever came into my head, no matter how meaningless. Her eyes remained closed, and she did not respond to my conversation in any way. I kept glancing at the kitchen clock, wondering when help would arrive. Every minute that passed seemed like ten.

Finally, I heard a siren's wail, and I rushed to our front door. An ambulance appeared in our driveway with its emergency lights flashing. Two attendants wearing white smocks and trousers, and white, lace-up shoes entered the kitchen. Kneeling on either side of Grandma, they checked her vital signs. One guy lifted Grandma's eyelid. Then he shone a pen light into her eye.

"Looks like a stroke," he told the other attendant.

The two of them lifted Grandma onto a stretcher. They strapped her down with canvas belts. Then they rolled her out the back door and down the driveway. I followed them outside, listening to the crackle of their radio while they slid Grandma into the rear compartment of their ambulance.

Two hours later, Mom and I sat in a waiting room at our county hospital. A young doctor in a lab coat emerged through double swinging doors. A stethoscope hung about his shoulders, and purple crescents appeared beneath his eyes.

"She's suffered a cerebral aneurysm," he told us. "A blood vessel in her brain burst. It has affected her speech and memory. Right now, she can't use her left arm or leg."

My mom cursed, while I shook my head. Grandma, an invalid? I couldn't believe it. She'd always been so vibrant and active. The thought of her lying in bed all day, or sitting in a wheelchair, seemed incomprehensible.

When Mom asked if we could see Grandma, the doctor grimaced.

"She's resting right now," he said. "Why not come back tomorrow, during visiting hours?"

While I drove us home, Mom sat in the passenger seat; she gazed out her window, saying nothing. The slash pine forests we passed by looked dark and mysterious. Croplands were littered with dead cornstalks or the shriveled remains of cotton plants already picked clean of their bolls.

I kept waiting for Mom to lose control and weep, but

she didn't. She seemed more irritated than sad. I found Mom's lack of emotion curious. Just how much did she love Grandma, anyway? Did she even *care* that Grandma was sick? In all the years we'd lived in Cassadaga, I'd never seen Mom and Grandma hug or kiss or say, "I love you," to each other. There seemed to be an unwritten rule—an understanding in our household—that displays of affection were *verboten*. The most I ever got were kisses on the cheek on my birthday.

Was it that way in most families?

Maybe the reserved nature of our home explained my need for affection from other boys; maybe I was love-starved. Or maybe not. Maybe some sort of genetic sickness ran in the males of our family. After all, both Devin and I craved sex with other guys, although we had grown up in separate households. Maybe I was just a pervert.

By the time Mom and I reached Cassadaga, the sun had set. The western sky was hemmed in shades of crimson, gold, and green. Clouds on the horizon looked like blue battleships. In the pines and Sabal palms, crickets chirped.

My heart leapt into my throat when I pulled onto the driveway.

Jacob sat on our front porch, on the glider sofa, his overnight bag and basketball beside him, a book in his lap. In all the day's excitement, I'd forgotten he would spend the night this evening—the first time since our camping excursion at the spring. He wore a sweatshirt, jeans, and high-top sneakers. His hair grew over the tops of his ears.

While Mom prepared dinner for the three of us—canned soup and turkey sandwiches—I sat beside Jacob on the glider sofa. I told him about Grandma and all that had happened earlier.

"Should I leave?" he asked. "Do you and your mom

want to be alone right now?"

I shook my head. "Please, stay."

In the kitchen, little was said over dinner. While Jacob and I did the dishes, my mom retired to the parlor; she switched on the television to watch *The Jackie Gleason Show*.

I scoured a pan with a Brillo Pad, making circles.

I asked Jacob, "Has your mom ever hugged your grandma? Does your mom hug you?"

Jacob looked at me like I was daft.

"People in my family can't keep their hands off one another. Why are you asking?"

When I explained how things worked in our household, Jacob shook his head.

"I can't imagine."

Out on the driveway, we played one-on-one under the glow of the gooseneck fixture, both of us sweating. The game took my mind off Grandma; I got into a rhythm and played better than I normally did, even executing a few underhanded layups.

"You have the hot hand tonight," Jacob told me.

Sometime after midnight, we ascended the stairs to my bedroom. We took turns showering and brushing our teeth—me first, Jacob second. When he entered my room, his hair was damp. His towel was wrapped about his waist. I lay on my bed in my briefs, leafing through a *Sports Illustrated*.

My belly fluttered when Jacob tossed his towel aside. Naked, he rummaged through his overnight bag, looking for clean underwear. After he slipped into a pair, he stood before my bureau mirror, combing his hair with his back to me.

I moistened my lips.

"Look," I said, "we have spare bedrooms. You don't have to sleep with me; I'll understand."

Jacob twisted at his waist to look at me a moment. Then he returned his gaze to the mirror; he adjusted his part with the comb.

"I'll sleep in here," he said.

Moments later, we lay in darkness, staring at the ceiling.

"It's sad, what you told me," Jacob said.

"What's that?"

"The way your family behaves—the lack of affection."

"It's all I've ever known," I said.

Jacob ruffled my hair with his fingertips.

"Turn onto your side, Ty. Face the wall."

My heart thumped when I did. A shiver ran up my spine when Jacob draped his arm across my chest and pulled me to him. I felt the warmth of his chest against my shoulder blades. His knees pressed against the backs of my knees. His toothpaste-scented breath tickled the hair on the back of my neck.

"Sleep well, Ty," he whispered.

CHAPTER TWENTY-NINE

Basketball season ended when February did. Our record was 13–2, earning us first place in our conference and a trip to the district tournament, where we lost by three points to a high school from St. Augustine.

On a warm Saturday in mid-March, Ebersole hosted a post-season barbeque at his home, near the Stetson University campus in Deland. A ranch-style, cinder block home with a well-tended yard and an in-ground swimming pool, it seemed the sort of property beyond most school teachers' salaries.

When I asked Hartmann about it, he told me, "Coach married money."

Ebersole showed us his gentler side that afternoon. He stood at the barbeque grill, flipping hamburger patties and turning hot dogs, and trading recollections of our season with his players. He sipped from cans of Budweiser. Wearing a Banlon shirt, pressed chinos, and buckled leather sandals over argyle socks, he looked so different from the guy we were used to: the grouch with the whistle and the snarl.

An ice cooler held a gaggle of soda bottles: Coca-Colas, 7-Ups, and Dr. Peppers. A table, draped with a red-checkered cloth, offered a variety of foods: bowls of potato salad, baked beans, and coleslaw. Jars of Kosher dill pickles and banana peppers sat beside baskets of rolls. Other baskets cradled potato chips, pretzels, and donuts.

Curvaceous and graceful, Mrs. Ebersole had hair the color of Jacob's. Her eyes were emerald green. She wore a strapless sundress; it showed off her cleavage and shoulder blades. A diamond the size of a Chiclet glinted on her left hand.

Over the course of an hour, Ebersole introduced his wife to each of his junior players. When I shook her hand, she said, "It's a pleasure to meet you, Tyler."

She had met the senior players before, it seemed, as she greeted each by name. And despite the fact she hadn't attended a single game this season, she knew every player's position and his stats, including mine. During the party, most every guy on the team, and Mike Monroe as well, stole glances at Mrs. Ebersole; they gazed at her legs and ample breasts.

The Ebersoles' swimming pool was heated. We'd all brought bathing trunks and towels, and now we splashed about the pool, taking turns springing from the diving board, doing cannonballs, jackknives, and backflips. I couldn't keep my eyes off Jacob. His body was sleek and muscled. His suit clung to his buttocks like a second skin, and I longed to touch him.

When it came time to eat, all team members gathered in a semicircle on the pool deck, seated on folding lawn chairs, and balancing plates of food on our laps. Ebersole stood before us, hands in the pockets of his chinos, his gaze traveling from one face to the next.

"Gentlemen, we've had a great season. And you know why? It's because each of you has risen to the challenge I threw in your face, starting at tryouts and continuing through Districts. You never quit pushing yourselves.

"I'm especially proud of our seniors: how they've

performed, and the example they've set for our junior players. I can't tell you seniors how much I'll miss you next fall. It's been a privilege working with you, these past two years."

I looked over at Hartmann, just in time to see him wipe a tear from his cheek. A couple of other seniors cleared their throats, while they stared into their laps.

Ebersole's gaze fell upon me for a moment. "Juniors, I'm proud of you guys, as well. I've seen remarkable improvement in your performances, and that's because you've worked so hard. You've given me everything I could ask for, at every practice and every game."

Ebersole wagged a finger. "Now, don't you juniors get cocky. When you show up next fall—and I'll expect each of you to return, no exceptions—I will work you just as hard as I did *this* season; you can count on it. Between now and then, I want you to practice every day. Every morning, get your ass out of bed and run two miles. Work out with barbells, eat right, and stay away from cigarettes. I want you fit and ready to play next fall. Do all you juniors hear me?"

Seven voices, mine among them, said, "Yes, Coach."

"We're not just a team, gentlemen; we're a family. Don't ever forget that."

Ebersole turned to his wife, and then he spoke in the gentlest tone I'd ever heard him use.

"Sweetheart, these boys look hungry. Will you please say grace so they can eat?"

CHAPTER THIRTY

My grandma never left the hospital. She died in mid-April, after suffering a second stroke. And while her death saddened me, I thought it a blessing in some ways. Each time I visited her, she was unable to speak, and I wasn't sure she even recognized me. She lay in bed, staring at the ceiling and not saying anything. The left corner of her mouth sagged, and her left arm hung motionless on her blanket.

I'm sure she was miserable.

Grandma's funeral was held at Colby Temple in Cassadaga. Rev. Hagermann presided over services. Every medium in town attended, along with many of Grandma's devoted clients. Some came from places like Atlanta, Montgomery, and Nashville. I hadn't been to a funeral since my dad's death, back in Decatur, and I found myself squirming in my seat while I stared at Grandma's flower-draped coffin. A soloist warbled, and a pianist played a somber melody.

As usual, my mom shed no tears at the service or at any other time, as far as I knew.

A week after Grandma's burial, Mom moved into Grandma's bedroom. She boxed up all of Grandma's clothing and shoes, and then took them to the Salvation Army in Deland. At her instruction, I carried all of

Grandma's diaries to the backyard, where I doused them with kerosene and set them ablaze.

"Who'd ever read them?" Mom said.

While Grandma's diaries burned, I studied the flames and thought of all the memories that were disappearing into smoke, right before me. I felt a tightness in my chest, a lump in my throat. I felt as though Grandma were dying a second death just then. And then I thought of *my* diaries hidden in my bedroom closet. No one had ever read them but me. If *I* were to die, would anyone bother looking at them, or would the diaries simply find their way to the Volusia County dump? Who knew?

Mom kept a few of Grandma's jewelry items—her pearls and diamond wedding ring—but the rest Mom pawned.

Mom's emotional detachment from the whole situation bewildered me. It seemed as though she was trying to erase any memory of Grandma from her mind. Every time I turned around, she'd thrown something else in the trash barrels: books, five dozen decorative spoons Grandma had collected during her travels, photograph albums, you name it.

One rainy afternoon, I stood before the Chevy in our garage. The hood was raised, and I cleaned corrosion from the Chevy's battery terminals, using a wire brush. Glow from a utility light illuminated the engine compartment. The time was around five thirty, when Mom pulled into the driveway in her Dodge Dart, her brakes squealing like cats in a fight.

Mom approached in her beautician's dress. She carried a sack of groceries in the crook of one arm, and rain droplets glistened in her hair.

"Mom," I said, "you need new brake pads."

She raised a shoulder. "I may buy a new car. I'm tired of driving that rust bucket."

Looking up from my work, I made a face. "Where would you get the money?"

She shifted the grocery sack from one arm to the other.

"Your grandmother had life insurance, fifty thousand dollars. A check came in the mail yesterday."

Her statement stole my breath.

Fifty thousand dollars? We're rich.

Mom's gaze traveled around the garage. She shook her head.

"This place is a mess. It's so crowded with junk, you can barely move in here. Do you think," she said, "someone might buy Grandpa's tools? Or should we throw them out?"

I winced. Devin and Jesse had used those tools while resurrecting the Chevy. And now *I* used them all the time, to maintain the Chevy. How could we get rid of them?

"Mom," I said, "please don't do that. I need these things to work on my car."

She didn't say anything; she only tapped a toe.

Anger boiled inside me. Mom was dumping everything related to her past, as though she couldn't wait to escape from it. Would she eventually get rid of *me*, as well?

Go on: say something.

"Did you even love your parents?" I asked.

She swung her gaze to me and scowled. "Of course I loved them. What kind of a question is that?" Her voice had an edge to it.

"Then why are you getting rid of all their things?"

She drew a breath, let it out. "You can't live in the past, Tyler. Besides, I may sell the house, once probate's finalized. I've never liked Cassadaga; you know that."

My knees wobbled. "Where would we move to?"

"Somewhere on the coast: Ormond Beach, or maybe New Smyrna."

"What about school? This fall's my senior year."

Mom looked at something over my shoulder, then back at me.

"They have high schools over there. You can transfer."

I thought about Jacob and my other friends at Deland High. I thought of the team and Coach Ebersole, and how disappointed he'd feel if I didn't return in the fall.

"Can't we stay here 'til I graduate? It's only one more year."

Mom lowered her gaze and didn't say anything. She only shifted her weight from one leg to the other.

"Mom, please, it's important to me."

She looked at me and pursed her lips.

"We'll see, Tyler," was all she said.

CHAPTER THIRTY-ONE

Sunlight glanced off the Chevy's hood ornament when I reached Deland's city limits, on a Sunday morning. I passed a used car lot, one festooned with strands of multicolored pennants. The pennants hung limp in May's breezeless torpor. Shops were closed, and sidewalks were devoid of pedestrians.

In a few minutes, I would pick up Jacob at his home. We'd play a two-on-two pickup game with Mark Maggert and Charles Sweeney. Ebersole had lent us a key to Deland High's gymnasium, so we could practice there instead of outdoors, where the heat was stifling.

I turned onto New York Avenue, whistling a tune. I felt happy and carefree, but when I swung my gaze to the Rexall store, my jaw sagged and my eyes bugged in disbelief.

What the hell?

A fire truck and pair of sheriff's cruisers were parked at the curb before the store. Mr. Rachinoff stood on the sidewalk, conversing with two uniformed deputies. All the Rexall's windows—and the front door as well—had been smashed. The deputies and Mr. Rachinoff stood amidst hundreds of glass shards; the shards glittered like diamonds on the concrete. I braked in the street and peered out the Chevy's passenger window. An acrid smell of smoke hit my nostrils.

Inside the store, everything looked blackened. A pair of firemen, their helmets reflecting sunlight, coiled a fire hose, while two others stowed gear in their truck's storage compartments.

I called out Mr. Rachinoff's name. When he saw it was me, he strode to my car and stuck his head inside. His forehead was furrowed, and his eyes were bloodshot.

"What's going on?" I said. "What happened?"

He scratched his beard and scowled. "Someone set my store on fire, Tyler."

I made a face.

"I don't understand?" I said. "Why would somebody do that?"

Mr. Rachinoff shook his head. "You'll see when you pick up Jacob."

At the Rachinoffs' home, chaos reigned. Their picket fence had been torched; it looked like a row of rotten teeth. A charred wooden cross lay on the front lawn, next to an empty kerosene can. Using red spray paint, someone had written "KIKES" in foot-high letters, several times on the walls of Jacob's house, on the flanks of Mr. Rachinoff's Plymouth too. The Plymouth's tires were flattened, its rear window was smashed. Again, an acrid smell of smoke hung in the air.

I joined Jacob on his front porch. We both crossed our arms at our chests while we surveyed the damage. Jacob wore blue jeans and a pajama shirt. He was barefoot. His eyes were bloodshot, and his voice sounded husky when he spoke.

"It happened early this morning, just before sunrise. I woke up when I heard glass shatter. I went to the living room, to look out a window, and flames were everywhere. He pointed to the cross lying in the grass. "The bastards lit that thing on fire, along with the fence. I didn't see their faces, but I saw them drive away—four men in a pickup truck."

I shook my head.

"Are you okay? Are your folks all right?"

Jacob shrugged.

"Yes and no. No one was injured, but my mom's pretty upset right now. Sorry, but I'll have to skip the game. I'm needed here."

I nodded. Then I told Jacob what I'd seen on New York Avenue, minutes before.

He shook his head while he sucked his cheeks. "I don't understand," he said. "Who would do this? And why?"

At the Sinclair station, the day after the fires at the Rexall store and Jacob's home, I found Cletis in the lube bay, smoking a Chesterfield and listening to an afternoon baseball game. Above him, a Ford Fairlane sat on the raised hydraulic lift. Cletis checked the gear oil level in the car's differential while we talked.

"School's done in three weeks," I said. "Can I have my job back?"

Cletis bobbed his chin.

"I can sure use the help," he said. Then he pointed to a row of cars parked at the edge of the station's apron.

"I'm backed up a week. Business is hopping, ever since that Deltona place opened up."

Cletis spoke of a real estate development in west Volusia County. Two brothers named Mackle were creating a city where none had ever existed—an endless expanse of cinder block homes built on tiny lots, all with a two-car garages and spindly palm trees in their front yards. Prices were low, financing was easy, and the homes sold as fast as the Mackle brothers could build them.

When I asked where Blon was, Cletis puckered one side of his face and shook his head.

"Mr. Numbskull broke his arm Saturday, playing touch football; he's out for a month, at least, and it couldn't have come at a worse time."

"I can work Saturdays," I said, "'til school lets out."

Cletis bobbed his chin. "That'd be swell, Slick."

When I tried telling Cletis about the Rachinoffs' troubles, he raised a palm to my face.

"I've heard all about it. Those Ku Kluxers are a bunch of goddamned knuckleheads."

"So it *was* Mr. Teague's people?"

Cletis shushed me. After looking left and right, he spoke *sotto voce*. "You can be sure of that, Ty."

I lowered my voice too. "Does the sheriff know?"

Cletis drew on his Chesterfield. Then he blew a stream of smoke.

"I imagine he does, but that doesn't mean he'll arrest anybody. This is Volusia County. One of those arsonists could've been an off-duty deputy, for all I know."

I chewed my lips and didn't say anything.

Cletis pointed his wrench at me.

"Listen, I know that Jewish boy's your friend, and that's fine. But don't get yourself involved in this mess. Steer clear of it, understand?"

I stared at my shoes and nodded while a sense of bewilderment crept over me.

The Rachinoffs were nice people. Okay, they were different in some ways, but they certainly didn't deserve this sort of treatment, did they? I thought of Byron Teague and Butch Delay, and then I thought of Lee Harvey Oswald. How could these people treat others so cruelly and so brutally? And what sickness had forged their peculiar brands of hatred? Did they take pleasure in committing their crimes? One day, would people like that turn their anger toward me?

CHAPTER THIRTY-TWO

Classes at Deland High ended the first Friday in June. On our way to the school parking lot, Jacob and I stopped by the gymnasium, to say goodbye to Ebersole and to wish him a good summer. We found him in his office, seated behind his desk and sipping from a Coke bottle. Monroe leaned against a wall, scribbling something on a clipboard. Ebersole wore a gray T-shirt, damp in the armpits. His whistle hung about his neck.

When I knocked on the doorjamb, and he saw it was us, a grin spread across his beefy face.

"Gentlemen," he sang out, "come right in."

Joining his hands behind his head, Ebersole leaned backward in his swivel chair. "What brings you here today? If you're looking for money or women, there are none here."

We explained.

"Well, that's mighty sweet of you two boys," Ebersole said. He brought his index finger to his chest. "I'm deeply touched." Leaning forward, he placed his elbows on his desktop. Then he pointed two fingers at us.

"Fuckspan and Jackinoff, I meant what I said at the barbeque: stay fit this summer; practice every day. I'm counting on you guys next fall. And don't you *dare* tell the newcomers what a sensitive guy I am. It's our secret, understand?"

Jacob and I looked at each other and grinned.

"Yes, Coach."

In the Chevy, while I drove us home, I told Jacob of the conversation with my mom. "She wants to move us to the coast," I said. "I'd hate to let Ebersole down, but the decision's not mine."

Jacob cleared his throat. "If that happens, you won't be the only one who'll disappoint Coach."

I shot Jacob a glance.

"What do you mean?"

"We're leaving Florida. We'll move back to Skokie, as soon as the insurance claims are in Florida are settled. Then we'll immigrate to Israel, probably next winter."

Israel?

My stomach churned. My hands shook so badly I had to pull the Chevy onto the road shoulder. After shifting into park, I rested my forehead against the steering wheel.

Jacob was leaving me? How could it be?

Jacob put a hand on my shoulder. "I'm sorry, Ty. I know you're disappointed; I'll miss you so much. But my family can't stay here, not after what happened. You can understand that, can't you?"

Tears leaked from the corners of my eyes. Why was life so unfair? Everyone I'd ever cared for had left me: Devin, Eric, even Grandma. Now Jacob would go, and I'd have nothing left but my mom and our hollow relationship. If Mom and I moved to the coast, I'd start my senior year at a strange school, not knowing a soul.

What could be worse?

Byron Teague parked his Fleetwood beside the Sinclair's gas pumps. I stood in the shady coolness of the lube bay—I was fixing a flat tire—and I grimaced at the thought of servicing Teague's Cadillac in the brutal afternoon sunshine. After leaning the tire against a wall, I strode onto the apron and greeted Teague, while wiping my hands on a rag.

Teague dipped his chin. "Fill her up, Junior, and gimme the works."

Teague strode into the station's second bay, where Cletis added Freon to a Buick's air-conditioning system. The two shook hands, while I approached the Fleetwood, squinting at the brightness of the day. I twisted off the Fleetwood's gas cap. Then I looked all about me.

No one was around.

I glanced at Teague and Cletis; they conversed in hushed tones. Cletis continued working while Teague stood with his hands on his hips, his back to me.

Do it. Go on...

After seizing a jug of sterilized water—the one we used to fill car battery cells—I emptied half the jug's contents into the Fleetwood's tank. Then I topped off the tank with gasoline.

I whistled while the pump ding-dinged; it sounded merry as a Christmas sleigh.

Right before Jacob's family left for Skokie, I took a day off from the Sinclair station. This was a muggy, breezeless Tuesday, in mid-July. By noon, the temperature had risen into the mid-nineties. A cloud of dragonflies hovered in our yard; their gauzy wings fluttered as quickly as turning fan blades.

I sat on our front porch, reading the *Jacksonville Times-Union*, while sweat beaded on my upper lip.

Out on the street, Jacob's dad pulled his Plymouth to the curb. A body shop had repainted the flanks of the

Plymouth, to cover up the Klan's epithets, but the shop hadn't made a good match between the new paint and the Plymouth's original finish. Now, it looked like a former cop car.

Mr. Rachinoff waved hello. I waved back, while Jacob leapt from the Plymouth. He strode up our walkway, swinging his overnight bag, sunlight reflecting in his auburn hair. He wore a T-shirt with a Boston Celtics logo on the chest, blue jeans, and basketball sneakers. He carried his ball under an arm—a leather NCAA model like mine.

After Mr. Rachinoff pulled from the curb, Jacob plopped onto the glider sofa. He twirled the ball on his fingertip.

"Up for a little one-on-one?"

I shook my head.

"It's too stinking hot; I have a better idea."

Jacob crinkled his forehead.

My pulse accelerated when I spoke of the spring, a place Jacob had visited only once, on the night we'd made love in my tent.

"The water's nice and cool," I said.

"I didn't bring a swimsuit," Jacob told me.

"Don't worry," I said, "you won't need one."

A half hour later, I stretched apart two courses of barbed wire. Jacob ducked his head and slipped between them. Then he held the wires apart for me. We trudged down the pine forest path, crunching needles beneath our sneakers, each of us with a towel slung over his shoulder. I carried a rolled-up blanket under an arm—the same blanket I'd seen Devin and Jesse make love on, so long ago. Sunlight dappled Jacob's head and shoulders.

Neither of us spoke much. Jacob's impending departure had lent a somber feeling to the afternoon. We hadn't said so, but we both knew we'd never see each other again, once the Rachinoffs left for Skokie.

This was it for Jacob and me.

My thoughts turned to the afternoon I'd first brought Devin to the spring, on the day he'd arrived in Cassadaga. Doing a quick calculation in my head, I realized it had been nearly three years since I'd met Devin. Where had the time gone? So much had happened since then: Devin and Jesse's affair, Mom and Devin's scheming, my affair with Eric Rupp, Devin's marriage to Rev. Patterson, Jesse's suicide, Coach Ebersole, my first basketball season, and the torching of the Rexall.

I wasn't the same person I'd been when I first met Devin, was I? Physically, of course, I was different: I'd grown eight inches, put on thirty-five pounds. But I'd grown emotionally as well. I wasn't the naïve kid with his *Green Lantern* comic books anymore. I'd become well-acquainted with the peculiar nature of humans: their secretiveness and treacheries, their gullibility and foolishness, their lusts and bigotries.

And their cruelty.

Basketball, I knew, had played a major role in shaping the person I now was. The sport had instilled confidence and self-discipline in me. Under Ebersole's merciless training, I had endured physical and mental discomforts I'd never thought I could survive, and I'd come out tougher because of it. A desire for achievement, I now knew, dwelt deep within me. I craved my peers' respect, on the basketball court and in the classroom. And I had satisfied my craving through hard work and self-discipline.

Then there were the cars in my life: Dad's Super 88, the Chevy, Mom's Dodge Dart, and all the models I'd serviced at the Sinclair station. I'd learned much about them in recent years, first from Devin and Jesse, and then from Cletis and Blon. I had acquired a practical skill—car repair—one most people didn't possess.

"No matter where you go in this world," Cletis told me, "you'll always find work. There's a garage in every town; there are car dealers in every city. They'll always need a guy to twist wrenches."

No, I wasn't a kid anymore.

Now, Jacob and I stood on the banks of the spring, removing our clothing and draping items over the fallen pine's trunk. The tree's plated surfaces, once rust-red, had darkened with age. Now the bark was the color of a chocolate bar.

Jacob shed his jockey shorts, and then my mouth grew pasty. The sight of his naked physique and genitals made my belly do flip-flops. How beautiful he was, and how I longed to touch him.

After slipping into the spring, Jacob submerged himself. Then he rose to the surface. He stood in the waist-deep water while goose bumps sprang out on his pale skin. Clasping his biceps, he shivered like a little kid. His hair was plastered to his skull, and sunlight reflected off water droplets on his shoulders.

Looking at me, he squinted in the bright sunshine.

"The water's cold," he said.

I stood naked on the bank, flexing my fingers.

"You'll get used to it," I said.

I waded into the spring myself, feeling its coolness steal over me. After bending my knees, I submerged myself and listened to the sound of bubbles rising to the water's surface. Then I rose and jerked my head; I slung wet hair out of my eyes.

Jacob studied treetops while a chorus of cicadas hummed in the surrounding undergrowth.

"Have you ever run into other people out here?" he asked.

"Never," I said. "It's the most private place I know of."

I told him about watching Jesse and Devin make love here. I spoke of having sex with Eric Rupp at the spring, so many times.

"It's a special place for me," I said.

Jacob's gaze met mine. His arms were still crossed at his chest.

"I wish I weren't leaving, Ty. I'd like to spend summer with you."

I nodded. "It would be so nice."

Jacob moistened his lips; he studied the spring's glittering surface. "Do you think it's possible for two men to love each other?" he asked.

My pulse quickened.

"Yes," I said, "I do."

Jacob raised his chin, and then he looked at me again. Already the sun had partially dried his hair, causing it to lighten in color.

"Do you love me?" he asked.

I nodded.

"I feel the same about you, Ty."

Jacob extended his arms toward me. "I can't leave without touching you," he said. "I need to hold you one last time."

When I look back on my life, I know making love with Jacob at the spring was a magical event, one of the few I've experienced in my life. His beauty, tenderness, and passion thrilled me to no end. For a brief time, Jacob and I became one person instead of two, and when it was over I didn't want to let him go. I wanted to feel him inside me forever.

At that moment, if someone had asked me, "Did thee feel the earth move?" I would have answered, "Yes, I did."

After we dressed, we walked upon the needle-strewn path, and sense of fulfillment rode through me, unlike anything I'd experienced before. I felt whole. I felt utterly at peace with myself, and with the world. I wanted nothing other than Jacob's presence.

I stole glances at him while we passed through patches of sunlight. I tried to memorize everything about him: his hair and milky skin, his bumpy, freckled nose, his long limbs and compact buttocks.

How would I stand living without him?

CHAPTER THIRTY-THREE

My senior year, I made first string on Deland's varsity squad. I played forward and co-captained the team, along with Mark Maggert. I averaged fourteen points per game—not bad, really. My peers elected me senior class vice-president. I made National Honor Society with a 3.6 grade point average, and earned myself a scholarship to University of Florida. My tuition, books, and housing—even the food plan—would all be paid for by the state.

In January 1967, I received a letter from Jacob, postmarked Tel Aviv.

Israel's much different than Florida or Skokie. It's arid and warm, with ancient architecture. Living in a place entirely peopled by Jews is strange, but I like it. It feels like home. I go to school at a yeshiva, like in Skokie. Everyone here speaks Hebrew, and though it was hard for me at first, I'm used to it now.

Because I'm eighteen, I've started military training on weekends, learning how to shoot and clean a rifle, how to fire rockets, how to march in formation and so forth. It's not bad. My commanding officer's okay, and I get along with my fellow soldiers. I've even joined a basketball club in my unit. We organize games, when we're not on duty. It's not like playing for Coach Ebersole, of course, but it's fun.

When I finish high school in May, I'll serve full-time in the army two years. Then I plan to attend the university, here in Tel Aviv.

My psychic powers had increased, along with my age. When I performed Devin's breathing exercise, I actually heard voices of the dead—Grandma's and Jesse's among them—speaking to me. But afterward I couldn't recall what they'd said. Why was that? Was I doing something wrong?

It didn't really matter. I had no plans to work as a medium—spiritualism wasn't something I found interesting—but if I concentrated, I could sometimes read the thoughts of my classmates and teachers. I often felt embarrassed when I explored their private worlds. So many harbored sexual secrets I would never have suspected. One male PE coach wore women's clothing on weekends, and my Calculus teacher cohabitated with her lesbian lover.

Using my psychic gift, I discovered certain boys at school fantasized about having sex with me. But I knew they'd never have the courage to do it. Girls at school flirted with me, but I never dated them—I had no interest—and after my moment with Jacob, at the spring, masturbation became my only sex life, my own private world.

On June 2, 1967, I walked across the stage in my high school's auditorium, wearing a forest green cap and gown; I received my diploma and the principal shook my hand.

"Congratulations, Tyler," he told me.

And that was that.

The first week of June 1967, war broke out between Israel and several Arab countries in the Middle East, including Egypt, Syria, and Jordan. No one was surprised. Tensions had mounted for months beforehand.

As my history teacher had said in class, weeks before, "It's not question of *if*, but only *when*."

The Israelis struck first, crippling Egypt's air force, and then stabbing into Arab territories on all sides of Israel. I watched the hostilities on the evening news—tanks screaming across parched desert—and I wondered where Jacob was. Was he part of the fight?

The conflict didn't last long: only six days before a cease-fire was declared. By then, the Israelis had reached the Suez Canal; they had seized substantial quantities of land, in both Syria and Jordan.

Then, during the third week of June 1967, I received another letter from Tel Aviv, this one with the name "Philip Rachinoff" written in the upper left hand corner of the envelope. I crinkled my forehead while I tore the envelope open. Why was Jacob's dad writing me?

Dear Tyler,

I'm sorry to inform you Jacob was killed while he manned a machine gun nest, near the west bank of the Jordan River. His mother and I are deeply saddened, of course. Jacob, as you know, was our only son. But we are proud he died fighting for his people and his nation.

During his time in Florida, Jacob always described you as his "best friend." His mother and I are so very grateful for the kindness you showed Jacob, when we lived in Volusia County. One day, I hope you'll come to Israel. Together we shall visit Jacob's gravesite.

In my mind's eye, Jacob's face appeared. I saw his freckled nose, his hazel eyes, and his auburn hair. I saw his lips, the ones I'd kissed.

My hands trembled, and my knees turned to jelly. A

teardrop fell from my cheek, onto Mr. Rachinoff's letter, and the tear diluted a bit of the ink on the page.

Oh, Jacob...

CHAPTER THIRTY-FOUR

On a Saturday in mid-July 1967, the temperature hit ninety-five. Heat waves rose from the asphalt street before our house. I sat on the front porch glider, sweating, with a *Newsweek* magazine resting in my lap.

I was working for Cletis again, but this day the Sinclair station was closed for installation of new pumps.

At loose ends, I felt bored and restless. What could I do? The day was too warm to shoot baskets. If I drove the Chevy to Daytona, I could walk on the beach, but the heat would make my stroll insufferable.

I thought of the spring and its cool water. Why not take a swim? Afterward, I could read beneath the shade of a slash pine.

I grabbed a blanket, the same I always took to the spring. Then I placed items in a grocery sack: a copy of Ayn Rand's novel *The Fountainhead*, a towel, a bottle of suntan lotion, and a jar of sweet tea.

After slipping through the lumber company's barbed-wire fence, I whistled as I followed the forest's footpath, crunching pine needles beneath my penny loafers. Like always, the woods smelled of sap. I spooked a deer, a doe. She dined on a blackberry bush, but when she saw me, she bounded off, kicking up dust. Her tail was a splash of

191

white among the forest's browns and greens.

The spring looked as it always had: clear and calm, its surface reflecting sunlight, its bottom white as table sugar. The only sounds were cicadas humming and, occasionally, a squirrel's bark. I spread my blanket on the pine needle carpet. Then I removed my clothing. It felt good to be naked in the sunshine and fresh air. I scratched my belly, wiggled my toes, and stretched my limbs like a house cat.

How I love this place.

The sound of a twigs snapping ripped me from my mental cocoon. I swung my gaze here and there, while covering my genitals with my hands. Who was there? What did they want?

Devin emerged from a stand of saw palmettos. He wore a chambray work shirt, blue jeans, and cowboy boots. His hair was longer than before—it covered the tops of his ears—and he'd put on muscle since I'd last seen him.

His lips parted into a grin when he approached.

"I thought I might find you here."

We shook hands. Then he stepped back and looked me over.

"You've grown since I left, Ty: in more ways than one."

Heat rose in my cheeks. I felt embarrassed, being naked before Devin, when he was fully clothed.

"What brings you to Cassadaga?" I asked.

He shrugged. "I'm only passing through." His hand went to a button on his shirt. "Mind if I join you?"

Moments later, we stood in the spring, our hair damp, water glistening on our shoulders. Devin told me he'd moved around since leaving Cassadaga: first to Savannah, then Charleston, then Atlanta. His last job was working in a municipal garage, maintaining buses and garbage trucks for the city.

I thought of Jesse, and how he'd made love with Devin at this very spot, so long ago. Then I thought of Detective Knox, and Jesse's ring with Devin's initials on it.

"I need to know something," I said.

Devin raised his eyebrows.

"Did you kill that girl—the one from Jacksonville?"

Devin shook his head. "That whole thing was Jesse's idea. He planned to collect ransom, quit the brickyard, and buy a car. He wanted us to live in California. But that girl was feisty; she nearly escaped, and Jesse had to strangle her."

Devin pointed a finger. "I *did* take advantage of the situation, Ty—it boosted my business—but that's all, I swear."

I nodded.

Then I said, "I have a gift: I hear voices, and sometimes I read peoples' thoughts. Do you, still?"

He bobbed his chin. "The spirit world exists, for certain. But it's elusive and hard to understand, isn't it?"

I said I had to agree. Then I touched Devin's bicep; I stroked it with a fingertip.

"Love can be elusive too," I said.

Devin looked at my finger. Then his gaze met mine and he crinkled his forehead.

"Do you want something from me, Ty?"

Unable to speak, I nodded instead. My entire body trembled.

"All right," Devin said. "You're an adult now; you're old enough to decide."

After seizing me by the shoulders, Devin pulled me to him, and then our hips pressed together. His mouth met mine, and our tongues rubbed. I thought of that morning, long ago, when he'd sat on my bed in his underwear. I had asked him for sex then, but he said no.

At last, it's happening.

An hour later, when it was over, I lay on my back on the blanket, with my legs draped over Devin's shoulders, and Devin inside me. I stared at the sky and blinked. A cloud, as fluffy and white as a cotton ball, drifted across the blueness, powered by a breeze that caressed my sweaty skin. Devin's cheek was pressed to mine, and I listened to him breathe while my heartbeat slowed. In the spring's surrounding undergrowth, the ever-present chorus of cicadas hummed.

Devin shifted his weight.

"Tyler?"

"H-m-m?"

"Are you okay?"

"Yeah, I'm fine. That was... beautiful, Big Brother."

Devin combed my hair with his fingers. Then he told me he loved me.

After we swam a second time, we dressed, and then I followed Devin to his Buick. He'd parked it on a road shoulder, not far from the barbed-wire fence.

"Where are you headed?" I asked.

"Miami. I have work there: mechanic at a Ford dealership."

I nodded. Lowering my gaze, I kicked red clay with the toe of my penny loafer.

Devin said, "You can come with me if you want, Ty. Just pack your stuff, and we'll go. We can build a life together—you and me."

I looked at Devin and sucked my cheeks. My eyes wiggled in their sockets. I didn't know what to say.

This is your chance, stupid. Take it. Each night you'll fall asleep in his arms; it'll be like a marriage.

Should I go?

I thought of my job at the Sinclair station, about my scholarship from the university, and how hard I'd worked to build a future for myself. Miami offered no opportunities—not for me anyway. I'd have Devin, but not much else.

And then I thought of a statement Devin himself had made, long ago: "Some things are more important than love."

Running away with him would not be sensible, would it? Wasn't it important to be sensible?

"I can't," I said, my voice cracking.

Devin puckered one side of his face, and then he nodded.

There on the road shoulder, we embraced, not caring when a transfer truck blew past, or when the driver honked and stuck out his tongue.

"You'll stay in touch?" I said.

"Of course. Miami's not that far from Cassadaga. Once I'm settled, I'll let you know where I'm at, and then you can pay me a visit."

I knew none of it would happen. I'd blown my chance, hadn't I? But now I performed my assigned role, as the naïve younger brother.

"I'd like that," I said.

Moments later, I watched heat rise from the asphalt while Devin's Buick rolled southward on the County Road. Sunlight glanced off the car's rear window.

"Bye, Devin," I whispered. "I love you too."

CHAPTER THIRTY-FIVE

It has been forty-five years since Devin came into my life and turned my world upside down.

My sophomore year in Gainesville, I met a boy named Andrew. We lived on the same floor in my dormitory. One evening, after drinking many beers, we became intimate. We fell deeply in love, and, after graduation, we lived together. I went to work for NASA, as an electrical engineer, while Andrew taught middle school English.

We lived happily.

My relationship with Andrew lasted twenty-one years, ending only when a pair of thugs murdered Andrew during a convenience store robbery. They shot Andrew in the face for no particular reason; death came before the ambulance arrived.

I've been single ever since.

My work at the Space Center interests me; I feel I'm part of something significant. The job pays well, and I like my co-workers.

My home on Merritt Island fronts the Indian River. I own a small sailboat, and often I'll take an early evening cruise. I'll troll a squid spoon, savoring Florida's sunshine and balmy breezes.

I have a basketball goal in my driveway, one with a

Plexiglas backboard. My neighborhood's full of kids, and sometimes I'll organize pickup games with a few gangly teenagers who don't mind playing with an old man, even if he's slow. I give them pointers on their ball handling and jump shots, and they always listen respectfully, because they're good kids.

I often think of Ebersole when I teach the boys. I'll wonder, *is Coach still alive?*

After the day Devin made love with me at the spring, I never saw him again. He did not call or write, and I had no idea where he lived or what he did. Then, in 1997, a Key West law firm sent me a certified letter. Devin, they said, had died from lung cancer. He'd left me his entire estate.

There wasn't much: a five-year-old convertible Ford Mustang, a bank account with a small balance, Devin's clothing, and several jewelry items—among them the signet ring with Jesse's initials on it.

Taking a few days off from work, I flew down there to sign papers. Then I drove the Mustang home, with Devin's possessions in the trunk. As I traveled the Overseas Highway, I studied azure waters. I thought of Devin, and all I had learned from him.

Tears streamed down my cheeks.

Why must life be so hard?

I still own the Mustang; I keep it in my garage. Sometimes I'll lower the top; I'll cruise the Interstate and my hair flutters like it did in Dad's Super 88, way back in Decatur.

When I lie in bed at night, sometimes I perform Devin's breathing exercise. As hard as I try, I can never connect with Jacob; I don't know why. Maybe Jews' souls dwell in a separate afterlife, one I can't make contact with. Who knows?

But I miss Jacob so.

Sometimes, I speak with Devin, my first love. He says he likes the spirit world. Compared to life on Earth, he says, it's carefree and effortless: no work or sickness, and no money worries.

"You'll see one day," he told me once. "We'll be together again. Maybe we'll play a bit of one-on-one."

Blinking tears, I asked Devin if a freshwater spring existed in the spirit world, one with singing cicadas, pine needles, and a scent of sap in the air.

"I'm sure there is," Devin told me. "We'll find one somewhere."

If you enjoyed *Tyler Buckspan*, you might enjoy reading Jeré's novel, *Josef Jaeger*, also available from Prizm Books. *Josef Jaeger* won first place in the Young Adult category of the 2010 Rainbow Excellence Awards, sponsored by the Rainbow Romance Writers association. *Josef Jaeger* also won Best Young Adult/Coming of Age novel in the 2009 Rainbow Awards, an international competition.

Josef Jaeger

Josef Jaeger turns thirteen when Adolf Hitler is appointed Germany's new Chancellor. When his mother dies, Josef is sent to Munich to live with his uncle, Ernst Roehm, the openly-homosexual chief of the Nazi brown shirts. Josef thinks he's found a father-figure in his uncle and a mentor in his uncle's lover, streetwise Rudy, and when Roehm's political connections land Josef a role in a propaganda movie, Josef's sure he's found the life he's always wanted. But while living in Berlin during the film's production, Josef falls in love with a Jewish boy, David, and Josef begins questioning his uncle's beliefs.

Complications arise when an old friend of his mother's tells Josef that his mother was secretly murdered by the SS due to her political beliefs, possibly on Roehm's order. Josef confides in his Hitler Youth leader, Max Klieg. Klieg admits he knows a few things, but he won't share them with Josef till the boy proves himself worthy of a confidence.

Conflicting beliefs war within Josef until he must decide where his true loyalties lie, and what he really believes in.

Jeré M. Fishback is a former journalist and trial lawyer. He lives on a barrier island on Florida's Gulf Coast. Visit his website at www.jeremfishback.com.

Tyler Buckspan

CPSIA information can be obtained at www.ICGtesting.com
Printed in the USA
LVOW06s2151030314

375935LV00012B/134/P